Bob Moats

I0567063

LIPSTICK MURDERS

By Bob Moats

Lipstick Murders

ISBN – 978-0-9903138-6-1

For information and address:
Magic 1 Productions
P.O. Box 524, Fraser MI 48026-0524
Website: http://murdernovels.com
Cover by Bob Moats

Bob Moats

Other Jim Richards series books by Bob Moats

For a preview or to purchase a book, go to
http://murdernovels.com

Lipstick Murders

What people are saying about the Murder novels by Bob Moats

"I went online this morning and read your book. I thought at first that I would only read a few pages, but got sucked into it and read all 11 chapters. You are a very good writer! I read quite a bit and often pick up "Airport" paperback mysteries to read on a plane. Most of them are dreadful, with obvious plots. Classmate Murders is a much better story than most."
Ray Zink, Entrepreneur, Minn.

"I got up to chapter ten of the Classmate Murders and decided then to buy the next two books." ... "Just finished your third book, the Dominatrix Murders. I thought it was the best one of the three, didn't want to put it down till I finished it. I looked forward to see how Penny would greet Jim every day after her show. Keep the books coming can't wait for the next one."
Norris, Retired Naval Corpsman

"Classmate Murders is well written and keeps the reader involved and wondering what will happen next throughout the book. Showgirl Murders keeps the reader involved throughout the story and keeps you guessing as to who the murderer is until very near the end."
G. Shurig, Kalamazoo

Bob Moats

"If you like mysteries and action then don't miss reading this book..."
Jan Schneider, avid mystery/crime reader

"Thanks for making me immortal, love the stories, your friend, Buck."
The real "Buck", George Carver

Extra special thanks to:

Special thanks to Val Brooks who edited this book and for her great suggestions.

Thank you to all the people who purchased this book. I hope you enjoy it as much as I enjoyed writing it for my faithful readers.

The Jim Richards Family of Readers is listed in the back of the book.

Lipstick Murders by Bob Moats

Chapter 1

The woman was reclined as her make-up was being applied. The foundation had been smoothed out on her silky skin and then rouge was added for color. Mascara was spread across her eyelashes, and then liner to bring out her eyelids. The person doing the make-up was looking through the various lipsticks in the make-up kit, to decide which color would make her look pouty and sexy. A deep shade of red was selected and applied to her lips. It was then smeared over her cheeks and finally the red was streaked over each eye. She now had a face that looked like the Joker from the Batman movie. She didn't care, she was dead.

~~*~~

I was relaxing in my office waiting for Lacey to come bombing in, telling me there was an emergency that needed my attention. She loved to startle me whenever a person came in looking for a private investigator. I had a good staff and associates, Trapper and Earl, both very competent investigators, but a bit goofy at times. It was something that broke up the tension of dealing with missing children or murder.

My good friend and business partner, Buck, took care of the security guard part of our business. He now had about a hundred and sixty men on his roster, all guarding various businesses in and around Las Vegas. I had moved my lovely wife, and now Vegas' favorite talk show host, Penny, out to Vegas to live. She fell in love with the town on our earlier visits. After we came out, Buck, Trapper and then Earl all joined us in Sin City. We left Michigan with all the snow and cold, for the hot, sunny life in Vegas. I never regretted the move. Neither did Penny.

I was suddenly startled by a tug on my pant leg. I looked down to see Willy, our toy Yorkie, pulling on my pant cuff. I smiled and reached down to pet him and pull him off my cuff. I hadn't seen him come into the room; he was so small and easy to miss. Now Penny wasn't so easy to miss, as she came in the office. She was a beautiful woman for her age. Not that I complain about age, I was now sixty-three and still feeling like thirty. Age doesn't mean a damn thing when you're trapped in an older body. Penny was a couple years younger, but looked like she was in her forties, and still sexy as ever.

"What were you daydreaming about?" she asked me, as she sat in the client chair at my desk.

"You in a bikini," I joked, as I looked to the poster of her in a bikini, on my wall. I had it made from a picture I took while we were on a ship cruise that resulted in murders.

Lipstick Murders

"I'm glad you have that poster, so you don't daydream about any other woman. Are you working on a case?" she asked.

"No, I'm bored here, thinking about going out for lunch. Want to join me?"

"I think you should wait for Lacey to tell you that there is a client in the lobby."

I was surprised about that, and wondered why Lacey hadn't called me yet. Lacey suddenly came flying in my door.

"Jim, you have a person out here and he needs help. I should tell you that he is hunky and handsome. He's a model!" she beamed and went back out.

Penny smiled and said, "I almost stayed in the lobby to watch his cute butt, but I saw Willy coming in here, so I followed."

"Cute butt? What's wrong with my cute butt?"

"Yours is cute too, but there's so much more of it." She smiled, as I stood.

"Are you insinuating I have a large butt?" I protested, as I headed towards the door.

"I'm not insinuating, I'm stating, you have a large butt."

I kissed her on the head and left the room. She followed on my heels.

I went through the glass doors to the lobby and saw him, he was hunky and handsome. I hated him right off. "May I help you?" I asked Mr. Wonderful.

Penny went behind him in the lobby and I could see she was checking out his body. He was wearing a red t-shirt and tight white jeans. I gave her a look and she smiled back to me.

"Mr. Richards, you were referred to me by a former client of yours, Stacey Trent," the Adonis said.

I cringed hearing the name, remembering her from the Black Widow murders. Her husband was killed by the spiders, and then we suspected her of the crime. She later proved to be innocent, but she was still a wacko.

"I remember her well. Shall we go to my office to talk?"

He followed me and then I pointed out my door, stopping to block Penny from following.

"You don't need to be in there. Go bother Lacey or something," I said as I went to the office, watching her in the hallway giving me dirty looks. I smiled to her, waved and closed the door. I knew that was going to bite me in the large butt later.

"Now, you are?"

"Barry Polander, I'm a model for the Lansome Modeling Agency. I do photo shoots for men's clothing and runway work when needed."

"So, why do you need a private investigator?"

"Actually, I don't. I need a bodyguard. I understand that you have people who protect celebrities."

I wondered how he figured he rated as a celebrity, but he must have money, so I wouldn't feel bad taking some of it. "Yes, we do have bodyguards to watch over celebrities. Why do you feel you need one?"

Lipstick Murders

"Have you seen the news this morning?"

"Sorry, I haven't seen the newspaper yet, or watched TV. What was there that I should know?"

"Tiffy Blumquest, the runway model, was murdered sometime last night. And threats were made to other models. I'm not taking chances, so I came to you."

"I see. I'll have to talk to a couple friends of mine on the LVMPD about the murder. How soon do you want to start?"

"As soon as possible, I have a career to think about, and I make good money at it."

I liked hearing that. "Okay, I have a person who would do well for you," I said thinking about Angelo, my former mob enforcer friend, who moved here from New York and started working for us. "He's someone who will not let anyone near you that you don't want."

"Is he tough?"

"Let me just say he used to be a leg breaker for a mob family out in New York. Is that tough enough?"

He got a big smile and said, "I like that. I'm from New York, would I know of the family?"

"Traviano, does that ring a bell?"

His eyes went wide, "Wow, yes. When do I get to meet him?"

"Hold on," I said as I went to the door and out. I went down to Buck's office and found Angelo relaxing in a chair on the side of the room. Buck was behind his desk doing paperwork, which he hated, but it had to be done. Angelo saw me and stood.

"Mr. R, good ta see ya dis morning." He was breaking back into his pattern of mob talk. Then he smiled and said, "I'll rephrase that, how are you this morning?" he grinned. "I'm trying to refine myself, I am rubbing elbows with famous people now."

I knew his job had put him guarding a number of really big celebrities who came to visit Vegas, so he had to project a better image.

"Angelo, you sound very refined. I have a case for you, if Buck has nothing else for you?"

Buck spoke, "You can have him, I've got nothing."

"Thanks. Follow me then." He came out after me and to my office. We went in and I introduced him to Barry. They shook hands, as Barry was looking surprised at the size of Angelo.

"Good to meet you, Barry," Angelo said. "You need protection, from whom?" he said with perfect diction.

They sat as Barry explained the murder and his concern. Angelo sat listening and then smiled.

"No, problem. I won't let you get hurt in any way. But you have to listen to me when I give an order to do something, like get behind me."

"I can do that, I don't need to be murdered. Are we good to go?" Barry asked.

"Sure, just stop on the way out to give the retainer to my receptionist and you can leave. You can be sure that Angelo is the man for your needs." I was sounding like a commercial.

They went out and I sat back in my chair as Penny came storming in. She closed the door and came over to sit on my lap. "Feel like fooling around?" she asked.

"In the office? How tempting. Or are you horny from seeing the Greek God?"

"Well, he may have given me the idea, but you know he could never replace you."

"I think you'd try. But there is no replacing me."

My door flew open and in walked Trapper. "Oops, am I interrupting something?"

"I think a closed door means that you are interrupting something," I said.

"Sorry, but I got a call from my gal Sam, she's invited me to go out of town with her, and I wanted to let you know."

"Okay, you've told me, now go and let us go back to what we were doing."

He went out and I reached over to my desk intercom and called Lacey. "Hold my calls and I'm now unavailable. Watch Willy and don't let me be disturbed."

"Okay, but you and Penny need to keep the noise down," she laughed and hung up.

*

Chapter 2

Penny did more fooling around than she did any serious damage to my body. "You're teasing me, aren't you? Just to get a rise out of me."

"Is it working?" she asked.

12

Bob Moats

I wasn't going to answer that if she couldn't tell. Lacey buzzed me on the intercom. I gave a dirty look to it and answered. "What did I ask you?"

"Not to disturb you, but you may want to come out here and see this," She said and hung up.

I carefully pushed Penny off my lap and stood, adjusting my crotch.

"Oh, I did get a little rise, eh?"

"Move, I'm needed," I said, and went around her to the door.

I came up the hallway and could see a number of women in the lobby, all beautiful and sexy. I probably would have to adjust my crotch again. I came through the glass doors and smiled. Penny came out behind me and stopped just behind me. I could hear her whisper, "Don't get any ideas."

"May I help you ladies?" I asked loudly, as they were all playing with Willy on the counter, making little baby noises to him. There were six of them, and they turned in unison as one came forward to say, "Mr. Richards, we need protection. Barry said you could help."

"He just left here not that long ago, how did he tell you?"

"Cell phone, he called me, and I told the girls. We have been threatened by some crazy person who killed poor Tiffy. Can you help us?"

I knew Buck would love this, "Lacey, call Buck in his office and have him come out here." She did.

"We just love your little dog," one woman squealed.

"Yes, his name is Willy," I replied.

13

Lipstick Murders

Suddenly one woman said loudly, "Oh, look, it's Penny Wickens!" Penny was still behind me and I was just about bowled over as they all rushed to meet her. "Miss Wickens, can I have your autograph," one asked and pulled a pad from her tiny purse. Penny was loving the attention and smiled to me. I just leaned against the counter and waited for Buck.

"Actually it's Wickens-Richards now. I'm married to Jim Richards."

"Who's he, a celebrity?" One blonde asked.

"No, he's just some guy I'm married to." She gave me an evil smile and signed their books.

I gave her the finger up the side of my head. She laughed.

Shortly after, Buck ambled out. His jaw nearly dropped when he saw the bevy of beauty in the lobby. But he maintained his cool.

One woman saw him and said, "Wow, he can guard my body anytime." Buck had this effect on women. He was tall, over six feet and very muscular. He was a biker back in his youth, so he developed a devil may care look about him. He came forward and asked me, "What can I do for all these pretty ladies?"

"They need protection," I answered.

"Well ladies, if you'll follow me and Mr. Richards. We can go to my office and talk."

I went to open the glass door as one woman passed by and asked if I was married to Penny. I said I was, and she giggled then went on. Penny came up and made a giggling sound and said, "Gee, Mr. Richards, you are so lucky to be married to Miss Wickens."

I just slapped her on her behind and said, "I have business to take care of, you can stay out here."

She laughed, picked up Willy and went behind the counter to Lacey's desk and sat next to her. I went to Buck's office where he had the women sitting and standing. I went to his closet and took out a couple folding chairs he had for when he had meetings with his men. I gave them to the women and they sat. I went up by Buck's desk and stood.

"Now ladies, are you wanting individual bodyguards or as a group?" I asked.

The one woman, who seemed to be the queen bee, spoke. "I think it would be advantageous to have individual guards. We don't all travel together."

"Good, we have bodyguards that can take care of all of you. I'll get them and have it set up," Buck spoke. He stood and went out the door to the back room where his guards lounged. He picked six of his men who had pulled bodyguard work before and had them follow him.

The men entered the room and the women were ogling them. Buck went to his desk and called everyone to listen up. "Now I'll assign the men to each woman. Who is going to represent the women for the fees?"

The queen bee stood and said, "The Lansome Agency is footing the bill, they have too much to lose if any more of us die. I'll arrange for their accounting to settle the fees."

"Very good, now I'll assign you each a man. Hmm, that sounds wrong in so many ways. But you understand."

Lipstick Murders

Buck took time getting the women and men hooked up as I went back out to the lobby. Penny was sitting with Lacey, as they were looking at some magazine.

"Good thing we have so much to do around here," I said.

"This is part of the job," Lacey defended. "This Las Vegas magazine has most of those women in it's pages. There's going to be a big fashion show next week and all the women are modeling. During the fashion show there's going to be a reality show taping to name the best model of the year. It's called "Greatest American Model" and will be on the Lifetime channel."

"Interesting, could be a motive for the murder of the model this morning. What's the prize?"

Lacey read the text and then said, "One million dollars and a contract to be host on a TV reality show about the fashion world. That's a good incentive to murder."

"Yes, it is. I need to talk to Lynn to see what she's got on the murder." I went back to my office passing by Buck's room, hearing all the giggles and chattering going on. Buck was probably in his glory right now, and so were his men.

I sat at my desk and picked up the phone. I wanted to call Lynn to get her take on the murder of the model, so we could plan better to watch the women in Buck's office. Lynn, and her now husband Deacon, had come back from Hawaii after their honeymoon. They were separated from each other in the police departments, Lynn still a Lieutenant in

Homicide and Deacon moved to Vice as a Sergeant. They had been our close friends since we came out here almost two years ago. Deacon came with us from Michigan and met Lynn, they fell in love and Deacon stayed.

The phone rang for a bit then Lynn answered, "Jim, what can I do for you?"

"Well, I have a whole room full of beautiful models, all wanting bodyguards from the killer of the model last night. Do you have any take on it?"

She paused, "They all came to you?"

"Yep, we are good at our job, so they want our services. Have you discovered anything that may help us to do our job better?"

"Do you have time to come down to the station?"

"Sure, I can be there in about twenty minutes."

"Good, see you then," she said and hung up.

I went back out to the lobby and told Penny I was going to LVMPD headquarters to see Lynn, if she wanted to come with me.

"Sure, I'll go. Lacey can you watch Willy?"

Lacey said she would and I went to Buck's office to tell him I was leaving.

"Okay, see ya later," he said, still surrounded by females.

Penny and I went out the back door to my van, and drove over to the station. We arrived and the officer at the door knew us by now and said to go through. We got to Lynn's office and she said to sit.

"How's it going Penny?" she asked.

"Good, you're still married and the baby still kicking?"

"Yep, it's going to be big like Deacon, I can tell."

"How much longer now?" I asked.

"Doctors say about four more months."

"I'm surprised Captain Weber hasn't put you on desk duty," I said.

"I am, but he's giving me a little latitude, told me to be honest about working Homicide or he'd pull me if I look like I can't take it."

"You have to consider the baby now," Penny said.

"I do. Now what is this about models attacking your office?"

I laughed and explained the morning to her. "Do you have anything that could help us to watch the women?"

"Yeah, be on guard for someone who does make-up."

"Okay, why?" I asked.

Lynn opened the folder in front of her and took out a couple pictures, then spread them on the desk in front of me. I moved forward and looked. It wasn't pleasant; the woman was made to look like a clown. Her throat was red from where I assumed she was strangled.

"Did she suffer or was it quick?"

"Joe Lang examined the body and said the make-up was applied after she was murdered. Made her to look this way. He said she died quickly."

"Where did this happen?" I asked.

"In her apartment, one of the other models found her early this morning. The killer also wrote on the wall, 'she's not the last to die' in lipstick. We're calling him, or her, the Lipstick Killer now."

*

Chapter 3

"Lipstick Killer? Have you talked to the make-up artists for the Lansome Agency? They must have a few for the models," I asked.

"I sent Greg Warren out to check on it. I didn't feel like being ugly around all the beautiful people. I'm going to have Deacon dig into it more tomorrow."

"Deacon? Why is he going to dig into it?" Penny asked.

"Oh, yeah, you don't know. Weber put him back in Homicide, to watch me. He's my safety net. I'm really hating being fat and pregnant."

"Where is he?" I inquired.

"He's standing behind you," came a deep male voice from behind me.

I looked back and there stood our favorite giant, standing in the doorway. "Deacon! Good to see you?"

"Good to see both of my favorite people. Hello Penny."

"Hi Deacon, are you getting nervous for the baby?"

"On pins and bowling balls," he smiled. "I'm the legs for Lynn now. I go into the field and bring her the info to catch the crooks. It works for me, and Weber. He's as nervous as I am."

"We'll have to make him the Godfather," Lynn added.

"Hey, I thought I would be the Godfather and Penny the Godmother." I protested.

"Jim you're sixty-six and would be dead before our baby would need to depend on you," she laughed.

"I'm only sixty-three, and have lots of years ahead of me. Weber isn't that much younger than I am."

"Don't worry about it, the time to decide hasn't arrived. Now can we talk killers?"

Deacon sat next to me and said, "Greg and I talked to the owner of Lansome Agency briefly, Kate Lansome, and she was in a rush to go to some meeting. She has an idea the murder was committed to prevent Tiffy from entering the competition. Then she rushed off. I'll have Greg and I pin her down tomorrow to explain."

"Okay, we have nothing so far," she said, then sat staring at me.

"What?" I asked.

"Since I'm restricted to my desk, maybe you could help Deacon to investigate. I have other crimes for Greg to investigate. I regret to admit it, but you seem to help out a lot."

"Seem to? I've helped with a good number of cases as a civilian consultant. I'd love to help on this case."

Penny snorted and said, "Sure, all those beautiful models, he'd be too distracted to figure out anything."

"Thank you my dear, I always keep my mind on the case, despite the suspect's appearance."

"Well, the models shouldn't be the suspects, since they were all threatened," Deacon added.

"One of them could be trying to get closer to the million dollar prize. Although, strangulation isn't really much of a method for a woman to commit. Men do most of that kind of crime," I said.

"True, but we can't rule out anyone. A determined model could garner enough strength to do the victim in," Lynn said sitting back in her chair, rubbing her protruding stomach.

"Uncomfortable?" Deacon asked.

"A little, I'll get over it. Now, you two go plot out the case, as Penny and I talk babies," she smiled.

Deacon stood and tapped my shoulder, "You don't want to be around when she talks babies. Follow me." He went out, as I stood and followed.

He led me to the breakroom, it was half full of people who probably should be working. Deacon offered me a Pepsi from the machine and made the selection. The can was semi-warm and flat. So much for precinct goodies. We sat by ourselves in a corner by a window looking out to the parking lot. Not a pretty sight.

"So what have you discovered on this case?" I asked.

"Not much, the owner of the modeling agency said she thought the model was murdered because she was a front runner to win the competition for Greatest American Model. The purse was a million dollars, and hosting a national TV show. What woman wouldn't want to knock off the competition?"

"So we get the pleasure of interrogating beautiful models," I said with a grin.

"Don't let Penny or Lynn hear you say that, or we'll both be put on desk duty."

"My lips are sealed."

"This looks like a person with some make-up abilities did this, so women or make-up artists would be our first to question. But I was thinking of starting with talking to the models. Shall we leave and begin our investigation?"

"Fine, I'll tell Penny we're going."

"How is she going to get back home?" Deacon asked.

"Ah, yes. Can you drive and she can take the van?"

"Works for me."

I went to tell Penny and she said that would be okay by her. "Just don't get too friendly with the women."

"Me? Get friendly? Not I."

"Yeah, you. If you're not home by six, I'm hunting for you," she said with a smile. "And with my gun," she added.

I waved to Lynn and went to find Deacon in the motor pool. He pulled the Dodge Charger Interceptor again, he really liked that car. Macho car, macho man. Damn, now I had the song Macho Man, by the Village People in my head. I found him as I hummed the song and did a few disco moves in the parking lot, he gave me a stare.

"Don't ask," I said as I got in the car.

We drove out to the strip and in to the parking lot of the Fashion Show Mall on Las Vegas Boulevard. Deacon managed to find a row of trailers behind one of the buildings, serving as dressing rooms for the big televised Fashion show. One trailer had a sign in big letters, Make-up, on its side.

Deacon parked and we went down the row of StarWagons, as the name stated on the end of each trailer. We came to the make-up trailer and Deacon went up the stairs. Suddenly a big man appeared at the door growling at Deacon, it was Angelo.

"Oh, Mr. Deacon, sorry I didn't recognize you at first. Hey, Mr. R. good to see you, too," the big man said, with a more pleasant smile than the grimace he had moments ago.

"Angelo, good to see you're on the job." I said.

"Yeah, Barry is in getting made up to walk the catwalk as they call it. They run shows here Friday to Sunday and Barry is participating."

Deacon went in past Angelo and stood looking at the row of chairs in front of well-lit mirrors. He turned to Angelo and asked, "Do you know who is in charge of all this?"

"Sure, Mr. David, he's the boss," then he whispered to us, "He's a little gay."

I whispered back, "There's no being a little gay, he is or he isn't."

"Well, then, he is. Not that it bothers me. He's the one in the pink slacks at the end of the trailer."

"Thanks Angelo," Deacon said as we went to the man having a fit about something.

Lipstick Murders

"I don't care if she wants to look pale, it's a bathing suit theme and she should look tan, so spray her!" The young assistant ran off as Deacon moved in front of Mr. David.

"Well, you are a big one," Mr. David said to Deacon.

Deacon showed his badge, and asked, "Can we go somewhere to talk?"

"Is this about Tiffy?" he said with concern in his voice.

"Yes, we're here to ask about the night in question. Now, can we go outside?"

"Of course, follow me." He went out and around to the side of the trailer. "Now, what can I do you for?"

"You can just answer my questions. That's all." Deacon was looking uncomfortable since Mr. David was giving him the eye.

"Very well, ask away," he said with a flourish of his hands.

"For starters, where were you last night between eight and midnight?"

"I was entertaining a friend, in my home. I can get you his name if need be, but we'd like to keep it quiet. He has a partner and he's a jealous type."

I could see Deacon was looking more uncomfortable, "Yes, his name please. We'll try and keep it quiet."

"Thank you so much, he's Perry Frampton. You know, like the singer?"

"Peter Frampton," I said.

"Yes, that one. Now don't go making a big deal out of it. Perry's partner is not a pleasant man."

"Is he dangerous?" Deacon asked.

"Oh God, no, he's just loud and annoying. So bitchy."

"We'll be careful asking Perry if he was with you. Do you have any theories about the murder?"

"Dear, all these bitches would have cause to murder Tiffy. They all want that gold ring on the ride to fame. A million dollars and a TV contract, that's a prize worth taking out the headliner of the show."

"What about the make-up that was applied to her face?" Deacon took out the photo from a folder he was carrying and showed it to the man.

"Oh, good God, this wasn't done by anyone who knows how to apply make-up. The eye liner is smudged and the rouge is too heavy. This was an idiot doing this. I'd fire anyone who'd do this. Poor Tiffy."

"Well, thank you for that. We may need your expertise again."

"Thank you, I'll be glad to help. Now I have to get back or all the bitches will take over."

He skittered off as Deacon looked to me, "That man makes me uneasy."

*

Chapter 4

"Why? Because he's gay?" I asked.

"No, because he's weird. I know gay people, they don't send me vibes like he does."

"Because he was showing an interest in you? I saw him flirting with you."

"Still has nothing to do with him being gay."

"Maybe he wants to spend some time with you, alone," I said with a smile.

"Knock it off, I'm not that way."

"Gay? You're the last person I would take for gay, or wanting to be with a man."

"My wife thanks you for that. Now can we get back on track here. We have a killer on the loose and we need to find him, or her."

"Good with me. Did you give him your number?" I grinned.

"You're really asking for it," Deacon said with a growl.

"No, I think he was asking for it," I said and walked away quickly, leaving Deacon standing behind the trailer. He followed, as I went up the stairs into the make-up trailer. I looked back to him and said, "Shall we go ogle some sexy women to prove our manhood?"

"Sounds good, I need to get my head back into sex with women."

"Don't let Lynn hear that," I said and went to a blond sitting in a chair getting made up. "Hi, what's your name?"

"Who's asking, creep?" she sneered.

I looked to Deacon, "Well, she's rude wouldn't you say, Watson?"

"Elementary, my dear Holmes. She is rather rude." Deacon held his badge up to her face, real close so she could see. "Now you want to answer Sherlock's question?"

"Sherlock? What kind of name is that?" she said, not fazed by the badge.

Deacon was getting a bit miffed, "How would you like to go with us handcuffed, in a patrol car to police headquarters to answer Sherlock's questions?"

She looked to her reflection in the mirror and said, "Okay, what do you want to know?"

"Name?" I said.

"Brandy Baker," she finally answered reluctantly.

"Well, Brandy, did you know Tiffy, the girl who was murdered?" Deacon asked.

"We all knew Tiffy. She was such a princess, always strutting her stuff, and acting like she was the Queen Shit around here," she said almost spitting.

I looked to Deacon, "Sounds like this girl could have had a problem with Tiffy. Maybe she's a good suspect for murder?"

She about came up out of the chair, "Hey, hell, I didn't kill her! I ignored her bitchiness, she was a whore for the runway."

"Explain?" Deacon asked.

Lipstick Murders

"She thought she was God's gift to fashion. She was good at the job, but she had an ego problem. There were a lot of girls who didn't like her, more than me. A lot more who would have liked to see her dead." She sat back and calmed down.

"Have any idea who may have wanted to kill her, besides everyone?" Deacon asked.

"Good question, Watson," I kidded.

"Thank you, Sherlock," he replied.

Brandy looked up to us and said, "You two are weird."

"Thank you. Just answer the question, ma'am," Deacon replied.

"What was the question?"

Deacon sighed, "Who do you think did it?"

"Easy, Lana Rule, she's the next princess to take over, now that the bitch is gone. She most likely did her in."

"And where would we find Lana Rule?"

"Out on the catwalk, and she makes the term fit. Meow."

We thanked her and went out to find Lana. I figured she'd be in the mall, on the runway. So we went there.

We moved through a long hallway from the back entrance that emptied into the mall. On the way, we passed a number of women and men running back and forth, probably all in the show. We came out by a new looking stage built with an extended runway for the models. On the back of the stage was an elaborate neon and LED lit sign announcing the big "Greatest American Model" competition. Behind the stage was erected a tent that was attached to the back of the stage. Probably where the models changed.

Deacon went to a flap opening of the tent where people were rushing in and out. He walked through the flap and into what was a chaos of movement and rushing people. There were about twenty persons moving about, it was hard to get a number since they moved so quickly.

"This reminds me of the day in the precinct, when we had the terrorist threatening to hit Vegas with the virus," Deacon laughed.

He stopped a frazzled looking woman with a clipboard, and quickly asked, "Where's Lana Rule?"

The woman gave him a scowl and said, "She's busy."

Deacon held out his badge, "Well, I can make her un-busy real quick. Where is she?"

The woman sighed and pointed to a blonde being dress by two men. "Give her a moment to do the walk and she'll be done."

"Thank you," he said and we went over to the side of the tent where she was screaming about how slow they were getting her ready.

"Move it you morons, I've got to get back out there!" she yelled loudly.

"Well, Watson, I'd say she has a temper."

"Indubitably, my dear Holmes," he came back.

"Indubitably? You've been using that word book Lynn got you."

"Undoubtedly so," he gave me a big smile.

Lana tore out of the tent towards the stage, as we went to the opening where we could watch her walk the walk. While the music blared, she strutted like some hot shit, stopped and did a turn, then stopped again. She gave a shocked look and then collapsed to the stage in a heap, covered by the gown she was modeling.

There were loud expressions of surprise from the crowd, as people from the show rushed to her. Deacon was out of the tent quickly and up to her, pushing people back. He was on his knees checking her, and saw the rivulet of blood from her side. He pulled his cell phone and made the call to LVMPD.

By now, security for the show had moved in and pushed people back. The leader of the security men knew Deacon and asked what was going on.

"Tom, get everyone in the tent to stay, and watch for a shooter in the crowd. See how many people you can find who may have seen anything," Deacon asked the man to do this for him.

Tom pulled his walkie-talkie and called for the rest of the mall security to get to his location. He called to his men around the stage and gave them orders. I was standing off the side of the platform watching it all go down. Deacon looked to me and shook his head, she had to be dead.

About an hour later, Lynn was standing by the runway watching the Medical Examiner's people, led by county coroner Joe Lang, wrapping the lifeless body of Lana in a bag. Penny was standing by me, on the sidelines.

"You saw this happen?" she asked Deacon.

"Jim and I were standing over there," he pointed to the opening in the tent, "I heard no shot, the music was too loud, or the killer could have silenced the weapon. CSI is going over the security camera footage, to see if he can see a gun flash. There were lots of people here, they didn't even jump when it happened. I guess they didn't figure there was a gunman in their midst and they didn't hear the shot."

"Who was she?" Lynn asked.

"Lana Rule. One of the other models told us she was expected to be the front runner for the competition."

"Yeah, well, she's out of the race now. We're getting a pattern here." She looked to me and asked, "Did Lana have a bodyguard?"

"I don't think I saw her with the women who came in for our services. But even if she was guarded, it would have been impossible to protect her out here."

"True, it took balls to kill her in front of all these people. Have you rounded up the people behind this circus?" she asked Deacon.

"They're all in the tent under guard by Tom Deluca and a few of his security guards."

"Tom Deluca? There's a name I haven't heard in a while. I knew he left LVMPD years ago, but didn't know he ended up here."

"Yep, he's the Captain now. Better than when he was a Sergeant on our team. Probably making more money now, too."

"Okay, let's go talk to these people. We may have to shut this thing down for the sake of everyone else." Lynn turned and went to the tent now being guarded by the security people. They let her and the rest of us pass, we went in.

There were eight people sitting around a table covered with props for the show. They all looked distressed and upset. Lynn went to them and asked for the head of the group. One woman stood and said she was. Lynn went over to her.

"Sit back down, please. I need to know what the hell is going on. Why are these people being murdered, in your opinion?"

The woman looked really upset, almost on the verge of crying. "This shouldn't be happening. This was supposed to be a fun competition and promote our products. Not become a murder fest."

"I understand, but why the murders?"

"They say it's a cut throat business. Now it's a murderous business. It boils down to money and power. Isn't that the main reason for crime?"

"Any thoughts on who may be doing this?" Lynn asked.

She replied simply, "Honey, it could be any one of these murderous bitches."

*

Chapter 5

"I don't buy it," I said as we left the tent.

"Why, Sherlock?" Deacon asked.

"Well, this was a very good kill shot, and all the bitches were in the tent or in the trailers. Besides, there was no make-up, so your lipstick killer is just a killer now."

"You really like to mess up my cases, don't you?" Lynn said, as she went to the stage where CSI was trying to get a handle on the shooting. "Anything, Dave?" she asked the supervisor of the team.

"From the security video footage we examined, she was facing the back of the stage, and was hit on her right side. So we deduce the shot came from high up, over there, upper level east, by Macy's." He was pointing up towards an area with potted palms.

"Could someone have brought a high powered rifle in amongst all these customers, and not be seen?" Lynn asked.

"Anything is possible. You need to check the maintenance people, video shows a couple were in that vicinity with cleaning carts, during the time of the shooting. A cart could have been used to easily carry the weapon. We're checking the palm plants for gun shot residue. I'll give you a call if we get anything."

"Thanks, I'll be back at my desk shortly. All this extra weight is slowing me down."

"Tough being pregos," he laughed.

"You bettcha," she replied.

An officer came up to the supervisor and said he was needed up on the level where they believe the shooting originated. Lynn, Deacon, Penny and I followed him up to the scene.

Dave saw his people standing by the huge potted palm plants and asked what they had. One of the CSI techs pointed to one of the huge square posts holding up the building, next to the plants. Everyone looked to the wall of the post, as he moved the palm branches aside and they saw it.

A smiley face made with lipstick.

Lynn looked to me and smiled, "Well, your theory is moot now. We still have a lipstick killer."

She turned to Dave and asked, "If you can get a make on the lipstick, it might help."

"Will do," he replied.

We stood looking down to the stage; it was a straight shot from here to the kill.

"He had to be a really good shooter to hit her with one shot," Deacon said. "Could be former military or cop, someone with the skill."

"Or a very good hunter. He stalked his victim and took the shot, while she moved along the runway," I added.

Dave spoke, "As I said before, we have video that there were custodial people in this area. Can't see their faces, so they knew where the cameras were."

"People?" Lynn asked.

"They weren't together, just being on the level at the same time."

"I'll need to know who they were and talk to them," she said to Deacon.

"I'll get on it," he replied, "after you go back to the precinct to rest."

"Isn't that sweet," she mugged, "touching concern for me."

Bob Moats

"I know you're able to handle this, but the baby doesn't need to be broken into crime fighting before he's old enough."

"Whatever, just find out who the people were and haul their asses in to be interrogated if need be."

"Now we discussed about language in front of the baby."

Lynn just stared at Deacon, shook her head and said to Penny. "If you want to go with me, we'll leave Sherlock and Watson to fight crime."

"Sounds good to me," Penny said and gave me a kiss on the cheek. "See you later, Sherlock."

I watched Penny going off with Lynn. I had to admit that Penny still had a rear end that turned me on.

Deacon asked Dave where the mall offices were. He called a uniform standing nearby and said to take us to the offices. We followed the fairly young man, who looked like he may be a rookie.

"Are you a new recruit, officer?" I asked.

"Yes, sir. Just out of academy, last month. I'm Frank Melkan," he said, and stuck out his hand to shake, we did. "I know who you both are, pleasure to meet you. I grew up here in Vegas and always loved watching the Metro Police working the streets. I applied and was accepted. I wouldn't mind making Detective someday."

Deacon laughed, "It's not all that glamorous, believe me. Just do your best, stay clean, and kiss a lot of butt. You may make it."

We went across the mall to where the mall offices were and Officer Melkan left us at the door.

Lipstick Murders

We entered to a high counter and the girl behind the desk asked if she could help us. Deacon showed his badge. The girl looked to it and said, "We've been busy with police all morning, this is about the dead model, I presume."

"Yes, it is. I need to speak to someone in charge of your maintenance and custodial department."

"That would be Bob Norton, he's in his office. Shall I announce you?"

"That would be nice, thanks," Deacon said with a smile to the young woman.

She called to say there were two police officers to see the man. She listened and hung up. "He'll be right out."

We thanked her and waited. About two minutes later and fairly large man came out of a hallway and motioned to us to follow. We went down the hall to an office that was huge. It had a couple desks and numerous people running around doing their work. Norton motioned to a couple ugly chairs by his desk and asked, "What can I do for you, officers?"

"That's Detectives, well, I am, he's a civilian adviser," Deacon said pointing to me, "We need the names of your people who were in the area at the time of the shooting this morning." Deacon handed the man a piece of paper with the information given to him by CSI regarding the location of the shooter. The man looked at the paper and then turned to a big board on the wall and studied it for a few. It had plenty of names, times and locations for cleaning and other functions.

"I had only one person in that area around that time. Ben Fossily, he was cleaning the trash cans. There were no others assigned there."

"Surveillance videos show at least two persons with carts were up there, around that time."

"Well then, someone else shouldn't have been there. I keep a tight ship and want to know where my people are at all times. There was only one person scheduled to be on that level at that time. If there was someone else, then it wasn't one of my people."

"Where can I find this Ben Fossil?" Deacon asked.

"Fossily, hold on," he turned back to the board and then said, "He's cleaning restrooms on this level, end of the court. Go out the door and all the way straight down. He should be in the men's or the women's right now."

"Thanks," Deacon said and we went out. We walked towards the restrooms, passing through busy tourists milling about, all going around in their own little worlds. They had no concern or idea about the murder that took place earlier. It was fairly crowded, I was sure that made the store owners happy.

We ended up all the way across the mall and found a sign pointing out the restrooms. We followed and found them. There was a cleaning cart in front of the men's room, blocking the entrance.

Deacon moved the cart aside, just as a man was coming out and saw us. "Hey, this room is closed for cleaning, you'll have to wait."

Deacon flashed his badge and said, "You Ben Fossily?"

Lipstick Murders

The man looked a little concerned and said he was.

"You were on the second level around the time the runway model was shot?"

"Yeah, I saw her go down, but I didn't know she was killed until later. I was watching all the babes on the stage, from the balcony."

"Did you hear a gun shot or see any other cleaning person on the same level?"

"I heard nothing, the music was blaring, but I did see one guy pushing a cart, but I figured he was new, I didn't recognize him."

"Could you describe him?"

"Plain, about my height, had a beard, and his cap was pulled low, so I couldn't really see much of his face. He had coveralls on so I figured he was one of us."

"What was he doing?"

"Same as I was, watching the show. But he moved away from where I first saw him, and then I didn't see him again."

"Do you have an extra cleaning cart sitting around now?"

"Yeah, as a matter of fact. It was left on that level by the restrooms. It should still be there, I wasn't going to move it, if the guy was too lazy to do it."

Deacon pulled his cell phone and called Dave to tell him about the cart. "It should be by the restrooms on your level. Check it out." He listened, then hung up.

"Thank you, Mr. Fossily. If you should see the man again, call me." He handed the man his card and we left him at the men's room door.

"I doubt he'll see him again, you do realize the shooter is long gone now?" I asked Deacon as we walked away.

"Sure, and we'll have to wait to see if CSI finds the cart and gets anything off it. Otherwise we don't have much else right now."

"Think we should go talk to the models some more?" I asked.

"Yeah, that's a good idea. Just don't tell Lynn and Penny," he said with a big grin.

*

Chapter 6

As we were walking away from Fossily, Deacon stopped and said, "I may still have a couple questions to ask Norton, so let's go back there."

We headed off again towards the custodial offices and entered. The woman at the desk called Norton and he came out. "Did you find Fossily?" he asked.

"We did, and he was right were you said he'd be. I have a couple quick questions; if the second man on that level wasn't one of your people, where would he have gotten the cleaning cart and uniform?"

Norton thought for a moment and then replied, "It wouldn't be easy, but we do have rooms throughout the building where we keep equipment, he could have pulled one of our spare carts out from there. As to the uniform, all our people have their own, we don't stock extras. If this guy did have a uniform, he would have had to have bought it from our supplier."

"Could you ask all your people to watch for a spare uniform that may have been stuffed in a trash can?"

"Sure, if it does belong to one of my crew it would have a name tag on it. That would help clear up the extra uniform." Deacon handed him his card and said to call if they find it.

We thanked him and left, heading back to the stage. We came up finding Dave and he turned to us and said, "We found the cart, they just brought it down." He pointed to the cleaning cart now being examined by his people. One of the techs was rummaging in the trash bag and pulled out parts of a sniper rifle, disassembled.

"Well, this is a break. He must have pulled it apart to take with him, but something stopped him. He just left it," Deacon said. "If you find any prints on it, let me know. Although I believe it probably was wiped clean."

"Or he wore gloves," I offered.

"Yeah, the cleaning people would wear gloves and not attract attention." He looked back to Dave and said, "Keep me informed."

We left the stage and went around to the tent in the back. There were two uniforms watching the opening. Deacon smiled and said, "Tough duty having to guard all these beauties?"

They both grinned and agreed. We went in and found Lynn and Penny talking to one woman standing by a makeshift table for make-up. We came up behind them and waited.

"That was the last you saw of our victim Tiffy?" Lynn was asking the woman. She didn't appear to be a model, she was too plain and was dressed in every day clothing.

"Yes, she left our trailer yesterday after we removed her make-up, she said she was going to her place to rest.

"Was there anyone giving extra attention to her? Some stranger or one of the people who work here?"

"Not that I noticed. Her manager was in talking to her earlier, but he left before she did."

"Manager? These women have managers?" Lynn asked.

"Yes, and some have agents. They all want a piece of the riches these girls make. But I'm sure her manager wouldn't kill her, she was worth more alive than dead."

"Unless she had a big insurance policy," I said to Deacon. Lynn heard me and looked back.

"Ah, the great detectives return. Have you solved the case yet?" Lynn smirked.

"We're hot on the heels of the killer, only time will tell," Deacon mugged back.

Lynn turned back to the woman and said, "Thank you for your time, I may need to talk to you again later." Lynn turned and led us off to the side of the tent.

"We talked to a couple air-headed models and they had nothing ground shaking to tell. The make-up people all agree that Tiffy wasn't made up by a pro. Did you get anything?"

Deacon explained what information we had gotten from the custodial people and that the rifle was found. Lynn felt that was good, and then said, "I'm hungry, anyone else hungry?"

We all looked to each other and agreed. "Let's go get something to eat then." Lynn said and headed out of the tent.

Deacon looked to Penny and me and said, "She's hungry all the time now with our kid on the way. I have to put up with her raiding the fridge at two in the morning."

"Pickles and ice cream?" Penny asked with a big grin.

"Worse, she wants sardines and bagels. I have to stock up on that crap, and I hate the stuff."

We heard Lynn yell loudly from outside, "Are you coming?"

"The hungry beast callith," Deacon grinned and went to the opening.

"I think we need to go back into the office and see if it's still standing," I said to Penny.

"Fine with me, all this beauty is getting me down," she replied.

"Oh, come on, you are as beautiful as any of these women, and could walk the walk with the best of them," I said with a grin.

"That earned you a few points, you can cash them in tonight." She walked to the opening and out. I followed, watching her rear. Still a nice sight.

I came to Lynn and Deacon both talking about where to eat. Deacon wanted something grilled, Lynn wanted a Gyro at a Greek restaurant.

I interrupted. "Guys, we're going back to the office, you enjoy your meal and we'll see you later."

They both said their good-byes and went back to arguing about where to eat. I smiled and led Penny out. Suddenly I stopped and asked, "Do you have the van?"

"Yes, I do. I wasn't going to let Lynn drive in her condition. We figured she could get a ride back with Deacon."

"Great, lead the way. You do remember where you parked?" I asked.

"Of course I do. I'm not senile yet, like you."

"I love you, too."

We spent about ten minutes trying to find the van, I was trying not to laugh for fear Penny would punch me. After about five more minutes we found it. I opened the door for Penny, she thanked me with a kiss.

I drove back to our office and parked in front. We entered the door to the front lobby and found Tracey smiling. "Hey, Mr. and Mrs. Richards, how are you today?"

"We're good. Don't you get lonely out here, closed off from the rest of the office?" I asked.

"No, actually I enjoy it. There's not much to do so I read books. I've read all of yours."

Lipstick Murders

"Flattery will get you everywhere with him," Penny laughed.

"Shall I announce you or are you going to surprise Lacey?" she asked.

"I like to scare Lacey, when she's not paying attention. Thanks, Tracey."

Lacey and Tracey, it was confusing sometimes, but they both were good workers. Penny and I quietly went through the front doors to the main lobby and found Lacey with her head down in a pile of papers busily working. Penny went to the counter first and yelled. "Hey!"

Lacey jumped up and gave a hard look to Penny. "It's bad enough that Jim pulls that crap, now you are doing it?"

"Sorry, I couldn't resist. Where's Willy?" Just as she said that, the tiny dog came running from out of the hallway and up to her. Penny picked him up and nuzzled him.

"It's been quiet in here since the bimbos all left," Lacey said with a smirk.

"Hey, they are clients, treat those bimbos with respect," I kidded.

"Whatever. Earl wants to see you when you come in. Are you in?"

"Do I look like I'm in?" I asked.

"I can never tell. You are here so infrequently."

"Well, I'll start hanging around more, just for you," I looked to Penny, "I'll go see what Earl wants and get back to you." I gave her a kiss and left her and Lacey to plot world domination.

I got to Earl's door, but stopped. I peeked in Trapper's office and it was empty. I turned back to Earl's office and went in. "What up, super spy?" I asked.

"Hey, you do exist. What have you been up to?"

I told him about the models and the killings. He sat listening and nodding like a bobble head. He did that a lot.

"So I missed the bevy of beauties? I need to get to work on time more. Now, I have a case that needs an extra eye. I got a call from an old friend and he is being accused of stealing corporate secrets from the company he worked for. They let him go because of it and may press charges for stealing. Are you busy on the model case?"

"Afraid so, I've already told Lynn and Deacon I'd help. Is Trapper busy?"

"I'll ask him whenever he shows up. You don't get paid for helping LVMPD do you?"

"Nope, but it's a favor that I can call back anytime I need it. Besides, I have enough money in my bank from my book sales to last me for a good number of years without being paid."

"Yeah, I still have a big nest egg from my sordid past with the CIA. We both could retire happily to our own island in the Bahamas. Now, poor Trapper will have to work until he drops," he said with a laugh.

"True, but I'd feel sorry for him and let him live on the island. But he'd have to get his own coconuts."

"Okay, I'll see if he wants to help on my case. Give him something to do."

"Give who something to do?" Trapper asked as he walked into the office.

*

Chapter 7

"Ah, the other prodigal son returns. You do know you work here?" Earl asked Trapper.

"I work harder than you. Paula seems to get most of your time." Trapper shot back.

"Oh, I suppose all the little vacations you and Samantha take, don't cut into your job responsibilities," Earl cut back.

"Before you two get to bare-knuckle fighting, why don't you marry your ladies and then you'll be able to get lots of work done?" I said.

They both gave me stares that suggested I might get pounded. "I'll just leave you to talk it out. Later." I left the room quickly, nearly running into Penny in the hallway.

"What did Earl want?" she asked me.

"He needed help with a case. I'm busy, so he's going to ask Trapper. Let's move along." I was turning her and pushed her gently down the hall to my office.

"Hey, slow down. Are you in trouble?" she asked.

"I suggested that Will and Earl get married."

"Why would they want to do that? They have girlfriends who might not like them marrying each other."

"No, babe, I mentioned they should marry their girlfriends, so they would have more time to do some work here."

"Are you saying marriage kills romance and they won't have to spend as much time as they do now giving their girlfriends' attention?"

I knew whatever I said would come out wrong, "No, not what I meant. We have plenty of romance, don't we?" I was ready to duck.

She just stood staring at me. I wasn't sure what she was planning. Then, she smiled, "I have gotten lots of romance from you. I like when you surprise me with flowers and candy."

I realized I hadn't done either of those things, so I had to change the subject quickly. "How would you like to go eat at Wolfgang's and then maybe take a walk around the Boulevard Mall? They have nice jewelry stores."

"Yes, very expensive jewelry stores. Shall we go?" She turned and walked out, still carrying Willy.

"This is going to be an expensive lunch," I mumbled and followed. "I should learn to keep my mouth shut."

As we went through the lobby, I yelled to Lacey that we would be back later.

"So, you're no longer in?" she said sarcastically.

"No, I'm out, and I will be out for the rest of the day, if I'm lucky." I turned away from her and went out the front after Penny.

Lipstick Murders

We drove to Wolfgang Puck's Bar and Grill in the MGM Grand and had a very nice meal. I was relaxing and said, "Remember our first visit to Vegas, we stayed right here in this hotel."

"Yes, and that's the time you took the first bullet that didn't kill you. I was happy for that," She replied.

I relaxed hearing that. "I wasn't very happy about it. That sucker hurt and I didn't like wandering around lost in the desert trying to get back to civilization."

"Well, you did find your way back. Now shall we go explore the Mall?"

It was inevitable, so I paid the bill, left a hefty tip and we went out. As we were getting into the van, my cell phone rang. I had put a ringtone on it that sounded like the old-type phones' ring. That annoying clanging bell sound, but it was so cool to watch people trying to figure out where the sound was coming from.

"Hello?" I asked, answering.

I put it on speaker since it was Lynn, "Jim, what are you doing right now?"

"I'm being punished. What do you need?" Penny smacked my arm and then picked up Willy.

"We got another body and Buck isn't happy," her voice came through.

"Buck? What's Buck got to do with it?"

"He was guarding the woman. He went to get her a cup of coffee, from next door at the coffee shop, and when he came back she was dead. I'm feeling really sorry for him, he's really angry. Could he do something dangerous?"

"Hard to tell with Buck, he may revert back to his biker days, but I hope he will take it well."

"You need to get over here, he's storming around the building. I think he's foaming at the mouth right now."

"Where are you?"

"At the Lansome Modeling Agency, on Charleston, corner of Maryland. Look for all the black-and-whites," she laughed and hung up.

I looked to Penny and said, "We'll have to go to the mall another time, Buck needs us."

"You lucked out on that, but I won't forget."

"Yes, Dear, I know you won't." I started the van and drove out.

We arrived at the building and went in the front door. There were uniforms all over the place, probably to ogle all the good looking models. We came in to find Greg Warren standing outside a door looking in.

"Hey Greg, what's up?"

I heard a familiar voice, it was Buck. He came out of the room looking about as mad as I have ever seen him.

"Jimmy, I want blood! You need to help find this fucker."

I took Buck's arm and pulled him aside. "Okay, I understand your pain, but calm down. We'll find the fucker, but you know it takes time."

"Yeah, the killer better enjoy that extra time he'll have before I tear him apart."

"Talk to me, what happened?"

Lipstick Murders

"I got too confident. I didn't figure she could be murdered in the office. I took over for Liston, the guard assigned to watch her. He had to take his kid to something at school. I was relaxing when she wanted a coffee, I went to get it next door at the coffee shop."

"Don't they provide coffee here?"

"Sure, if you like dog piss. She was a whiney bitch, but she was my whiney bitch. So I went to get her a good cup of coffee next door, and when I got back she was dead. She had lipstick smeared all over her face. Damn it!"

Lynn was standing at the door and said, "Don't blame yourself Buck, this guy was a pro. No way he could have slipped in and then out after the kill. He, or she, was here all the time. I got my people questioning everyone as to who was in the building, we'll narrow it down."

I turned to Lynn, Deacon was standing behind her. "This is getting to be too much. Too many quick kills in such a short time. If you pull the plug on the competition, the killer has no reason to murder any more women," I said.

"I said that, but the Mayor and the City Council has already put their two cents in. This show is bringing in mucho bucks to the city and the prestige of our town for the thing is important for the image. The Mayor is sympathetic, but he wants results to end this before the big show."

"Maybe he should investigate, see if he can stop the killer."

"Well, gee, Jim. You want to tell him that. I don't like the man, he puts the buck above lives. I'm not happy, so we need to get on with this and catch the killer."

Penny whispered in my ear, "Am I becoming a widow again?"

I grinned at her and said, "Don't worry, I'll give time to you, too."

Lynn went to the office where coroner Joe Lang was just getting ready to bag the body.

"Anything you can give me now, Joe?"

"Yeah, she was murdered," he smiled, as he zipped up the bag for his people to take out.

"Gee, it's good they keep you around for comic relief. Now what's your professional opinion?"

"Okay, the beauty was garroted with a wire. Thin and short, just enough to reach around her neck, judging by the thumb bruises on her neck by the wire scar. Easy to bring in, hidden in any number of places on a body and disposed of easily. CSI is tearing into the building looking for it. I don't think they will find it, but that's my opinion."

"You're just a fountain of information. Thanks Joe. Let me know if you find out anything else." Lynn turned to Deacon and said, "Shall we see if our people have found anything from their questioning?"

She went out followed by Deacon, Buck, Penny and me. She went down a hall to another office where Greg Warren was standing outside the door. "How's it going Greg?"

"So far no one saw anybody out of the ordinary. Everyone was here who belonged here. Except Buck's body guards."

Lipstick Murders

Lynn looked back to Buck and asked, "Are all you're guards kosher?"

"My people are all good, background checks and criminal records. They have been with me since I started the security business. No one was new recently."

Lynn went into the office where Detective Williams was talking to a woman. We stood outside the door as Lynn introduced herself and asked the woman, "What is your function around here?"

"Function? You mean what do I do here?"

"Yeah, okay, I meant that. What do you do here?"

"I'm a receptionist. I watch the front office and keep things running properly. It's not easy to keep all these women being where they should be."

"So the woman," she looked at the folder she had and continued, "Gerry Jenkins, who was murdered, where was she supposed to be?"

The woman looked a bit shaken and answered, "She was not scheduled to be anywhere else, she was just here in the building for a photo shoot."

"Where's the photographer?"

She paused, "Uh, I don't know. He was here earlier, then the mess with the murder came up and I didn't see him after that."

Lynn looked to Deacon and said, "Find the photographer."

*

Chapter 8

Nothing more could be done at the modeling agency, until they tracked down the photographer, so Penny and I left. I figured the photographer would be hard to find and I wasn't going to worry about it. Now Buck was another matter. He left with us in his own car and followed us to the office.

We arrived and parked in back. In the parking lot, Buck stood looking at the building. "What's going on in your head, Buck?" I asked.

"I started this security business, with your help, to make something of myself and my people. Today, I failed one person, who I was supposed to be guarding. I'm not happy about it."

"Buck, they slip through the cracks. We can't be everywhere and prevent everything. We just have to take it one day at a time. I understand your pain, but it's done and we need to find the killer to make it right."

"Thanks Jim, it doesn't change my feelings, but it helps. We need to find this bastard."

"And we will, just go with the program and follow the leads. We can't do much without the LVMPD doing the real leg work, but we can help, as we always have."

Penny was behind me with Willy, "Buck, you do what you can, but it never seems like enough. You'll be vindicated soon, I'm sure you will."

Lipstick Murders

"Thanks Penny. Jim isn't good enough for you; leave him and run off with me. We'll get away from all this insanity and live a happy life."

"Buck, you couldn't afford her," I said with a smile, just before Penny knocked it off my face. "Ouch, that was mean."

"Well, you're an idiot. I'm the best thing you've ever had. Now let's go in and see if Will and Earl have murdered each other."

"Or proposed." I said with a grin. Buck gave me a strange look and I said to not worry about it.

We came in the back door and I waved to the camera so Lacey would know we were in. We went to our respective offices and I sat at my desk. Lacey came to the door and said, "Wow, it's strange to see you sitting there."

"If you don't drop it, I'll put you out in the front lobby and bring Tracey in to do your job."

"Go ahead, I could use the vacation." She stood defiantly, I gave in.

"Okay, what is it you need?"

"You have a person up front who needs your help." She smiled and walked off.

I looked to Penny and said, "I'm not having a good day with women, am I?"

"No Sweetie, you're not," she replied.

I stood and went out to the lobby where I was surprised to see Laynie Keller, the well-known pop singer, sitting in the waiting area. She had a man with her and he didn't look happy.

"Miss Keller, it's a pleasure to meet you, what can I do for you?"

"You can protect me. I'm being threatened by some stalker, and I want it stopped," she said looking concerned.

I looked to the man, still sitting and asked, "And you are?"

"I'm Laynie's manager, Marty Brice. I'm concerned also about her safety. Your name came up in conversation with the police. They can't provide protection unless there's an attempt on Laynie's life. You were recommended."

"Well, I'm flattered that someone thought enough to send you here. Now if you'll follow me, I'll see what we can do to help you."

I knew this is what Buck needed to take his mind off the murdered woman, so I led them to his office. He was sitting at his desk staring at the ceiling when we came in. He sat up straight when he saw Laynie, and then stood.

"Well, Laynie Keller, it's an honor to meet you," he said rushing around his desk to pull a chair over for her. She thanked him and sat. Buck ignored the manager and sat on the edge of his desk by Laynie. "What can I do for you?"

"I have a stalker, and he won't leave me alone. Now he's making threatening statements towards me. I need someone to protect me while I'm here in Vegas."

"Is this stalker from Vegas?" Buck asked.

"Yes, he has admitted he was, I've never been bothered by him until I came here."

"Do you know who he is?"

Lipstick Murders

"No, he has sent anonymous messages to my hotel where I'm performing this next week. I can't work under these conditions, but I have a contract to fulfill. Can you help?"

Buck looked to me, then said he'd be right back. He asked me to follow him and we stopped in the hallway outside his office. "Jim, what should I do? I want to find the killer of the model, but she's Laynie Keller, I really want to guard her."

"Well, you could call Angelo in, I heard he was done with the male model," I said. "He could watch her so you can track down the killer."

Buck paused, looking distressed. "Sure, I want to find the killer, but that's Laynie Keller. I don't often get a chance to be around such a celebrity and a great looking one at that. She needs proper protection." He had a dilemma, I could tell.

"Jim, I need to ask you a big favor, would you find the killer for me?" he asked. I had a feeling he would.

"You got it, I'll take care of it for you. Now go work out the details with Laynie, she needs help and you need to keep a good eye on her."

"I'll even bring my own coffee for her. She won't be out of my sight for a minute." He gave me his trademark walrus smile and went back in his office.

I felt better now and turned, nearly running into Penny again. "Are you going to follow me around all day?" I asked.

"Until you take me to a jewelry store, then you're on your own." She kissed my nose and went towards the lobby again. It was hopeless. I went to Earl's office and it was empty, so went back to the lobby.

I asked Lacey, "Are Earl and Trapper off on a quest?"

"Yep, they're working a case, or so Earl said. Have you figured out who the killer is yet?"

"I'm good, not that good. Where's Angelo?"

"He was here after the hunky model had to go back to New York, but then he went to talk to a man about a empty restaurant on Flamingo. You told him you would front him to open his restaurant so he's working on it."

I almost forgot that I told him I would help. I could afford it and Angelo so wanted to have an Italian restaurant, I wanted to help him. "Have him see me when he gets back." I headed back to my office and felt Penny following me again.

I turned, "Okay, shall we go visit a jewelry store, just so you will stop tailing me?"

"I'm ready to go," she said, hugging Willy who gave a little yip in my direction.

"I'm not buying any jewelry for you, dog. You've got a nice collar now." I went to the intercom on my desk and told Lacey I was taking Penny out to deplete my bank account and then we started to leave the building, when Buck came rushing up.

"Jimmy, I'm taking the bodyguard job for Laynie. Can you warn Mac to watch the men?" he said breathlessly.

"Why don't you tell Lacey, she'll see him when she gets home, or she can call him," I replied.

Lipstick Murders

"Yeah, I forgot they were married. I'll do that." He turned and rushed off.

"I think Buck is losing it. His memory is getting foggy." I said to Penny and then we went to the van.

About an hour and $1,200 later, we arrived back at the office. Penny had to rush up to show Lacey her new necklace and earrings, and Willy's faux ruby dog collar. Now why would a jewelry store carry dog collars? I swear, Vegas is a crazy town.

I looked into Earl's office, still empty, and so was Trapper's. Buck was out with his favorite pop singer so I was the only one left in the office. I went to my desk and sat. I speed dialed Lynn and she came on, "What's up Sherlock?"

"Just calling to see how the case is coming?"

"Haven't found the photographer yet, he doesn't exist. And he left no equipment that we could get prints from."

"The shooting at the mall was by a man dressed as a custodian, the garroting of the model in the office was by a man masquerading as a photographer. I think we have a frustrated actor hit man. Maybe he was hired by someone to knock off the models?"

"It's a thought, all the kills were professional, especially the shooting at the mall. But I think any good hit man would know how to disguise himself. I haven't found one model who could even identify him. They all saw different things, he was ten different people according to them."

"Yeah, well, if they aren't looking at themselves in a mirror, they don't care how others look."

"How's Buck holding up?"

"I distracted him with a body guard job, Laynie Keller."

"Laynie Keller? How did she find you guys?"

"According to her, the police recommended us. Now wasn't that nice of your people."

"Hell, I would have taken the job, I love the way she sings. I'm sure Buck will be watching her closely."

"I'm sure, he was drooling when he said he'd take the job," I laughed.

*

Chapter 9

"So how many models are left to compete?" I asked.

"They tell us twelve women are still in the running. Three dropped out after the model was strangled in the office. They value their lives more than money."

"Or they didn't figure they would win. Either way, we have twelve women to watch. I'll talk to Buck and see what extra protection we can put on them. I'm sure the LVMPD doesn't want to incur the expense of manpower."

"Yep, the Mayor and city council are all for making money with this dog and pony show, but God forbid if we have to put out a few bucks to save lives.

Lipstick Murders

I presume Lansome Modeling is paying you, correct?"

"Yes, they are and paying well. I think I've had it for the day, I'm taking my wife home, along with the expensive jewelry I bought her today and getting a good night's rest."

"Jewelry? What did you say wrong that led to that?"

"I'm not even going to repeat it. I need to keep my mouth shut to keep from having to buy presents. I'll talk to you tomorrow, unless you find the photographer. Call me."

"I will, talk later," Lynn said and hung up.

I sat back in my chair just as Penny came into the room, still holding Willy. "Why are you just sitting there? Isn't there crime to solve somewhere?"

"No, my dear, I'm out for the night. Shall we go home so you can wear your new jewels to bed?"

"It's still early, shall we go eat?"

"All I can afford now is Sonic Burgers. We can't eat the jewelry."

"Sounds good to me. I'll tell Lacey we're leaving." She left my office as I stood, trying to get my body into a straight up position, I hated getting old. My parents always said that the body would break down, I didn't believe them. Now I know better. I was finding new things to ache about weekly.

I went out to the hallway, as Penny was coming back. "All's well up front?" I asked.

Bob Moats

"Yep, no beautiful women or hunky men now, just Lacey and Tracey hard at work. Now, the burgers await."

We left and had our meal, then went to our home on the outskirts of Las Vegas, overlooking the valley and the strip. I pulled into the drive and parked the van by the garage. It was too big to put in the garage, besides, my restored 1989 Crown Vic was in there along with Penny's car and the mini-limo. I probably should take the Vic out occasionally and drive it.

We went in and I had to shut off the driveway alarm and reset it. I figured we'd be in the rest of the night, but Penny said she was going to take a swim.

"I hope you're not going to wear your necklace and earrings in the pool."

"Do I look crazy. That's not accepted wear for swimming." She kissed me and went off to get changed. I yelled, "Why don't you go skinny dipping, I'll join you."

I heard her reply from the house, "If that's the only way you'll get into the pool, while I'm naked. I think not."

I went to the kitchen and put some kibble down for Willy, although he ate most of my burger at Sonic. I took a couple beers from the fridge and put one on the counter for Penny. I couldn't figure how she could drink one-on-one with me and not get a beer gut like I had. I really need to work on my figure, I looked as pregnant as Lynn.

An hour later, Penny was drying off, as I sat in a plastic chair next to the pool. I heard a noise to my left and it was Angelo coming through the gate.

61

Lipstick Murders

"Hey, old friend, what did you think of the restaurant?"

He came over and sat next to me. "Hey, Mrs. R., looking good."

"That's my wife you're ogling, Angelo," I said with a growl.

"Leave him be. I don't hear many compliments from you about my figure," she snipped.

"I have a dirty mind, so I keep it to myself," I defended.

"So Angelo, did you get the building?" Penny asked, as she sat with us.

"I liked it, but I want Mr. R. to look it over first. He's fronting the money, so he should have an interest in it," he said to Penny.

"Angelo, if you feel it's good, I'm fine with it. I presume the price is right and the building is not going to fall down?"

"Nope, all is good on that respect. Plus all the fixtures and cooking appliances are still there, so it wouldn't take any time at all to get ready to open. Just get a staff and food and I'm ready to go."

"Great, so get the building and start. I'll get you a check as soon as you give me a figure." I said.

"I'll get it to you tomorrow, as soon as I talk to the seller. It's a sweet little place, lots of atmosphere. An Italian treat with all the decorations. Plus the location is great."

"Well, put our reservations in for the first meal. And I expect superior service," Penny said.

"You got it, or I'll break a few legs." He laughed so loud and hard, I thought he would bust a gut.

"Sorry, I thought it was funny." He stood and said, "I'm going to call my Mom and tell her the good news. I may need some of her recipes for the menu." He went back out the gate to our guest house.

"I'm happy for Angelo. He's such a nice leg breaker," Penny joked.

My cell phone buzzed, and by the caller ID, it was Buck.

"How's the job doing?" I asked.

"Loving every moment of it. Laynie is a great gal," he replied.

"Don't let Maria hear you say that. I was going to call, we may need to provide more guards for the women, can Mac handle that?"

"Sure, he knows the system by now. Just tell him what you need and he'll handle it."

"Okay, I'll do that. How long are you going to be watching Laynie?"

"She's scheduled here at the Silver Slipper for a week, and then she leaves Vegas."

"Well, don't get in any trouble. The tabloids will have a field day with a scandal between you and her."

"I'm good enough not to get caught," he laughed and hung up.

Penny caught the gist of my conversation and said, "Maybe you should make an anonymous call to the tabloids and leak that Laynie and her bodyguard are having a fling. It may help business."

"Sure, and we'll have all kinds of women calling to get a piece of Buck. I don't think Maria would appreciate that."

Lipstick Murders

"You'd be safe, no one would want to have a fling with you," she said with an evil smile.

I stared for a moment and said, "You know, you are a mean woman. I don't know why I even put up with you."

"You'd be lost without me, and I keep you on your toes."

Now I had the evil smile, "I actually keep you around because you are great in bed."

She stood and pulled her bikini top up and off. "Put your money where your mouth is, Slick," she said breathlessly, gave me a wide smile and headed in the house.

I looked to Willy sitting on the ground. "Sorry puppy, you're not sleeping with us tonight."

I followed my sexy wife in and to the bedroom.

Thankfully, there were no calls in the night about killers or stalkers. I guess crime happens everywhere you go, but my curse of murder following me was still holding up. Three murders in less than two days, and a celebrity being threatened with death, my life was busy. Although I just usually stood around, giving my pearls of wisdom while LVMPD did most of the work. I was slowing down now, letting other younger people do the work, while I provided a little bit of brains. Not that I had many brain cells left.

I slept well, Penny had to get up early to go play TV host on her talk show. Willy was on the end of the bed watching me lay there. "What's on your mind this morning?" I asked him. He came running forward and started to lick my face. I didn't like being

64

licked by a dog, any dog, so I held him back. Now Penny could lick my face anytime and I'd let her.

She came out of her personal bathroom and was dressed to go face the viewing public. "Who's on your show today?" I asked.

"I think some strip hypnotist; he's been performing at the Planet Hollywood for a while. Do you want me to bring him home and hypnotize you into acting more like George Clooney?"

"Thank you, I thought you were going to say Brad Pitt. No I don't need to be hypnotized, especially after that case we had with the murderous hypnotist. Just leave him at the studio." I sat up on the edge of the bed and looked to her, "You know, I used to be terrified to come home, back when we lived in Michigan. I never knew what you were going to bring home from the studio to bug me."

"Yeah, I had fun in those days. Now it's all Vegas stuff, no silly things, like yoga or baking. I don't have anything unique to bug you with now." She stood looking at me, then said, "Give me a day or two and I'll find something to bring home." She kissed me and went out of the room.

I looked to Willy and said, "Now I'm in terror."

*

Chapter 10

Penny had left for work and I stumbled to the kitchen, in just my underwear, to get a couple pieces of toast and feed Willy. I stood watching the toaster burn my bread and heard Willy chomping on his kibble. My cell phone buzzed on the kitchen counter and I looked to see who was disturbing my morning, it was Angelo. I was surprised he was up so early.

"Hey Angelo, what's up?"

"You said to let you know what the seller wants, he said 200k. I hope that's not more than you wanted to put in." I could hear the meekness in his voice, which surprised me.

"No, that's actually less than I thought it would be. Are you sure there's nothing wrong with the place?"

"No sir, it's all good. I had a friend of mine who has a couple restaurants in town look it over. He knew the place from when it was open, but he confided with me that the owner wasn't a very smart business man, or restaurateur. He said it's worth more and I should take it."

"Well, you got it my friend. I'll cut you a check at work today, soon as I get in. Congratulations, you are now a restaurateur."

I could hear him make a small choking sound, a happy one. "Thanks, Mr. R. You are a prince."

"Thanks, see you at work." We finished and hung up. I stood looking at Willy sitting on the floor

66

looking up to me. "I'm now an investor in a restaurant. It could be the start of my empire." Willy yipped to me and I picked him up to go change into my clothes.

An hour later, I entered the building from the back, carrying Willy, and went to my office. Angelo was seated in my client chair and I had to grin that he was waiting for me.

"Morning, boss. Hope I don't seem too anxious?"

"No Angelo, I would worry if you weren't anxious. It shows you care. Now I'll get you that check and you can go buy your restaurant. I do expect a great meal when you open," I said, putting Willy on the floor.

"Yep, Mrs. R. already warned me about that."

"Yes she did, and you don't want to disappoint her." I said, as I took out my personal checkbook from my desk. I made out the check and gave it to Angelo.

"I added an extra seventy-five thousand so you can buy food, stock and hire people. You're going to have a long road ahead." It was actually a long road from when I first met Angelo and he did so much to help me catch criminals with his mob connections. He often talked about how he wanted a restaurant. Now it was happening.

"Thanks so much, Mr. R. I don't know how to thank you enough."

I could see the big man getting misty eyed, so I changed the subject. "Angelo, don't take this wrong, I'm glad I can help, but why didn't you talk to Gino about a loan?" I asked, referring to his stepfather, the capo of the Traviano Mafia family in New York.

"Mr. R., I knew my Mom would have made Gino's life miserable if I didn't get the money from him, but I didn't want a mob connection to my business. I wanted a clean break from that life, and you have given that to me. I am indebted to you."

"Angelo, Vegas was founded on the families of the Mafia. No one would have blinked if you went that way," I smiled.

"I know, but if word got out that the restaurant was fronted by the family, it would be overrun with every wiseguy who came into town. I want this place to be a nice normal family restaurant and not for a Mafia family." He gave me a big grin and stood. "Now I shall go take care of the paperwork and get my restaurant going."

"I never asked, what are you going to call it?"

"I'm calling it 'Mama Mia', Italian for 'my Mom'. I think she'd like that."

"You're a good son, Angelo. Now get out of here and go buy that building."

He gave me a salute and went out. I could hear him humming an Italian tune I recognized, as he walked down the hallway. I sat back feeling good.

Lacey came to my door and asked if I was in. I just laughed and said I was.

"Good, you have a person up front who wants to talk to you," she said.

"Who, may I ask?"

"She's with the models and is wanting to hire you."

"Have her talk to Buck or Mac, if she needs protection."

"She doesn't want protection, she wants a private investigator. Why she wants you, I can't figure out." She turned and headed back towards the lobby.

I yelled, "You can be replaced!"

"Go ahead, you'll never find someone as good as me!" she yelled back.

I figured it was useless to argue and went to the front, nearly stepping on Willy. He followed me.

I came through the lobby glass doors and found a rather plain looking woman, not exactly a model, standing at the counter. "May I help you?" I asked.

"Yes, Mr. Richards, I hope you can. Is there a place we can talk in private?"

"Of course, follow me." I asked Lacey to watch Willy and led the woman to my office. I pointed her to my client chair, as I sat at my desk.

"First, what's your name?"

"Betsy Parrish."

"Thank you, Betsy, now what is your concern?"

"I think someone I know is murdering the runway models. I need you to find out if he is."

I was a bit surprised that she told me this and asked, "Why haven't you contacted the police?"

"I don't want him to know I turned him in, if you take the case and find out it is him, he'll blame you and not me."

"Are you afraid of him?"

"Of course, why do you think I'm going to this extreme? I'm certain that he'd kill me if he knew I was even here."

69

Lipstick Murders

"Who is he?"

"Oh, sorry. He's Matthew Harden, of the Harden Agency."

"Okay, start at the beginning. Why do you think he's behind this?"

"I'm his personal assistant; he's a manager and agent for models. He's really a… pardon me… a prick. I tolerate working for him because of the money. I'm trying to help my mother get an operation she needs. It's personal."

"I don't need to know. Now, how do you know he's behind this?"

"I don't really. He represents Amanda Dawson, the model who is now in the best position to win, with the death of the other women. I heard some talk from Matthew and Amanda… I wasn't snooping… but could hear them talking. They were in his office and they were talking about the competition and how she was a shoo-in for winning. I only heard bits and pieces but he said he had taken care of the situation, and he was protecting his interest in her winning. He just sounded like he did the killing, or had it done."

"Okay, so far it's circumstantial, but worth looking into. It would make sense if he really wanted his client to win. That's a big prize and the contract for the TV show would keep him going for a long while. If you believe he thinks he's gotten his girl to the top of the pile, so to speak, I wonder if there will be any further murders. He can't kill all of them."

"From the way he was talking, I feel he thinks Amanda is safe now."

"Betsy, I think we really need to involve the police in on this. I have a friend in LVMPD who is discreet about matter such as yours. Would you be agreeable to talk to her?"

"I don't think so Mr. Richards. I really don't want him to find out."

"And he won't. But you know if we do find out he was behind this, he'd go to jail and you'd be out of a job."

She sat for a moment, thinking. "Crap, I didn't think about that. I really need this job, it doesn't pay well, but it's all I have."

"I'll see if I can help you with that too, now I can call my friend and have her come here to talk to you. Would that be all right?"

She paused, and then said, "Okay, but this has to be between us."

"I'll do my best to keep it that way. Can you wait here?"

She agreed and I went out to the lobby and behind the counter. "Hey, you're not allowed back here," Lacey growled.

"It's my company, and I'll go where ever I want. You're getting awful territorial lately. Now, I have to talk to Lynn and I want to use your desk, go take a break or hit the restroom. Just go away."

She made a laugh and stood, "Don't mess with my files." She left the lobby and went to the back. I sat and dialed Lynn on my cell phone. "Hey girl, I have a lead on the Lipstick killer. Are you interested?"

"I could be, what do I have to do?"

"Can you come into my office, I have a woman here who has an interesting story. The kicker is she doesn't want the person named to know she is the snitch. She's terrified that he may retaliate against her."

"I'll be right over, don't let her get away." Lynn said and hung up.

*

Chapter 11

Lynn and Deacon made quick time getting to my office. "Did you use flashers and siren?" I asked as I stood in the lobby waiting.

"Nope, just light traffic and a good knowledge of the back streets to take. Now what have you got?"

"Follow me," I said and took them into my office and I introduced Betsy to them. She was understandably nervous, "Betsy, please relax, Lieutenant Carter is on our side and will help to protect you."

"May I call you Betsy?" Lynn asked the girl as she sat next to her. I went back to my desk and Deacon sat in another chair off to the side.

"Sure, I hope you can find out if he killed the women. I don't care for the man but I don't like seeing innocent women being murdered for a stupid contest."

"Tell me everything that leads you to believe that you know the killer."

72

"As I told Mr. Richards, it's my boss, Matthew Harden, he's manager and agent for Amanda Dawson. She's one of the contestants in the Greatest American Model competition. She was ranked by the sports books and off casino bookies as a fourth place contender. As you know, the top three women have been murdered off, leaving Amanda in the lead now. My boss was talking to Amanda yesterday and from the small parts of what I could hear, it sounded like he had a hand in the murders. Maybe not him directly, but possibly someone he would have hired."

"Did he actually admit to killing anyone?"

"No, it just sounded like he may have had something to do with it."

"Well, being as he's one of the agents involved with the models in the show, we would have to interrogate him anyway. We just wouldn't have to mention that you were a witness to his conversation. But your statement moves him up the list of suspects. I won't mention that we got information from anyone, so you will be safe."

"Thank you. If he did murder those women, I'm sure he wouldn't hesitate to murder me."

"I want you to go back to work and pretend like nothing is changed. I presume we'll see you in the office and if you hear anything more, please let me know." Lynn gave Betsy her card. "Okay, go back to work. Hopefully, this will help us. Thanks you so much for coming to us."

Betsy stood and I got up to take her out to the front. After I saw her safely away, I went back to my office. "So, what do you think?" I asked.

Lipstick Murders

"It makes sense. I'll have to question him, under the pretense of questioning all managers and agents. He should buy that. Maybe I can make him nervous enough to say the wrong thing."

"If the women who were holding Amanda down in the rankings are all dead now, hopefully the killings are over," I added.

"I hope so. It's not looking good for the show to have all the women come up dead."

"If Amanda comes up dead, this is all going to be moot." Deacon said.

"Maybe we should put men on her, it may alter Harden's plans, causing him to screw up," Lynn said.

"Well, shouldn't we go talk to Mr. Harden?" I asked.

We had looked up his address and Lynn said she knew the building he was in. I went up to let Lacey know we were leaving, and told Lynn I would follow them in my van. We drove over to his office building and went into the lobby. I could see Betsy in the hallway off the lobby; she glanced at us, then went into a room off the side.

"We need to see Matthew Harden, please," Lynn told the receptionist, showing her badge. The woman got on her phone and called him. After she hung up, she smiled and said he'd be right out.

I was walking around the lobby looking at the numerous pictures on the walls of beautiful women. Harden had a nice selection of models to choose from. I saw one picture that had a label saying it was Amanda Dawson. She was good looking.

Matthew Harden came into the lobby from out of a hallway and gave us a big grin, "What can I do for our fine police. Is there a problem?"

Lynn stepped forward and said, "Three women were murdered and you're asking me if there's a problem?"

He looked a little shaken by her abruptness and asked us to follow him to his office. He led us down the hall to a room at the end. It was a fancy office, well decorated, with many pictures on the walls of more women.

"Quite an operation you have here Matthew… may I call you Matthew?"

"Of course, Officer."

"It's Lieutenant. Lynn Carter of homicide, and this is Sergeant D'Angelo and that person is Jim Richards, consultant to LVMPD. "

"Please have a seat, Lieutenant. What is it you need from me?"

"Just a few questions. We are interviewing all the managers and agents of the models in the Greatest American Model competition, about the recent murders of the three women in the contest."

"Yes, terrible stuff. Such a waste of beauty."

"A waste of life, any life, whether beautiful or not. Did you personally know any of the murdered women?"

"I had some connection to Tiffy, she was one of my models before she went to Lansome. It was an agreeable move, better for her. The other two I knew by reputation, but not personally."

Lipstick Murders

He was sitting with this really goofy smile, I didn't much like the man by first impressions.

"Any comment on why your model, Amanda Dawson is now in the forefront of the contest, because of the murders?"

"Just a fortunate stroke of luck I guess. Well... unfortunate for the victims." He paused, then got a strange look on his face. "You're not saying that Amanda had anything to do with the murders, are you?"

"Should we? Or maybe you had something to do with getting her the prime spot to win the million and a nice TV contract. You have anything to say about why we shouldn't investigate you?"

"Please, I'm not a murderer, nor is Amanda. It's just coincidence that Amanda has now moved up in the running to win. She's good at what she does, and would deserve to win."

"Where were you the other night when Tiffy was murdered? Between eight and midnight?"

"I was with a few friends, celebrating the opening of our east coast branch. We partied most of the night at the MGM Grand. I was with about twenty people, models and clients."

"I'd like a list of all those people, if you could. Just to rule you out. Was Amanda also at this party?"

"Of course, she's our premier model. She's our money maker, to put it bluntly."

"If she wins, it would mean more money for you, wouldn't it?"

"Lieutenant, I'm not liking the insinuations. This is a cut throat business, yes, but I'm not into murder to gain fame and fortune. I'm sorry, but I have a business to run, if you have no further questions." He stood and waited.

Lynn looked to Deacon and then slowly stood. "I don't have any more questions for now, Mr. Harden. I may have more later after we do a little investigating. Thank you for your time and I'll need that list of party guests."

"I'll have my secretary get it for you." He went around his desk and stormed out the door. We followed and he was gone. The secretary handed Lynn a sheet of paper, it was the guest list.

"Thank you," Lynn told the secretary. "Are any of Mr. Harden's models in the contest besides Amanda?" Lynn asked the woman.

"No, just Amanda. Between you and I, he doesn't really have many clients. Amanda and two others. They frankly couldn't walk the cat walk on all fours, if they tried. Amanda is his biggest asset."

"That's some strong words about your boss," Lynn said.

"I'm looking for another job. The sooner I can get out of here, the better. Harden is an ass and I don't like him."

Betsy came around a corner and looked surprised to see us still there. "Hello, and you are?" Lynn asked her.

"Uh… I'm Betsy. Are you the police?" she said, going along with the charade.

"Yes, we are. What do you do around here?"

"I'm Mr. Harden's personal assistant. More of a gopher, I should say."

77

Lipstick Murders

"Were you at this celebration party Harden held, the night Tiffy was murdered?"

"I was. As his P.A. I have to be in attendance."

"Was Mr. Harden there and was he there all night?"

"I think he was, I wasn't watching him," Betsy replied meekly.

The secretary snorted. Lynn asked, "You have something to add?"

"Harden was in and out with women, if you know what I mean, so he wasn't around much. They all think he can turn them into famous runway models. He couldn't turn Tara Banks into a famous model. He's a putz."

"Well, would you say he was capable of murder to get what he wants?"

"I'd say he'd do anything to get his women in the spotlight, as long as he could make a few dollars off of it," The secretary said, with a certain amount of hate in her voice.

I was watching Betsy and she seemed relieved that someone else was taking her side.

"I'm going to throw something out to you. Has Mr. Harden brought in here, or associated with, any men who look like they could be capable of murder?"

The secretary laughed and said, "He has friends who would kill for twenty bucks. They are all drug addicts and burnouts. Sure, if you think Harden hired someone to commit murder on the models, I'd say yes."

*

Chapter 12

Harden came rushing into the lobby from out of a side hallway and stopped. He made a grim face when he saw we were still there. "Betsy, come with me, I need you," he said and turned back down the hall. Betsy made a look of desperation and followed.

"Asshole," the secretary said.

"Can you give me any names of these lowlife associates that hang around Harden?"

She looked to the hallway and I moved over to look in, saying, "He's gone."

"Yes, I can. One was named Lefler, Mossa Lefler. He came in last week, just after the announcements were made from the sports book on the model contest. If I were you, I'd look into him. One other you can try is some guy Harden called Weasel, I heard him say not to call him that and Harden laughed and called him Darryl. Didn't get a last name, sorry."

"I'm sure we could track either of these men. Thank you so much for the assistance. If you hear anything that can help, let me know." Lynn gave the woman her card.

She thanked us and we went out. "Deacon, get with your Vice buddies and see if they have someone called Weasel, AKA Darryl, and this Mossa Lefler."

"I'll call as soon as we get back to the precinct. I don't like this guy, I think he's behind it."

Lipstick Murders

I said, "I agree, but you need to be alert if he thinks you know something. He seems like the kind of person who would do something desperate to cover his ass."

"True, let's see what we can find on the hoods before we do much more," Lynn spoke, as they headed to her car.

I went to my van after telling them I was going back to my office, and to call if anything develops. Just as I was driving out, I saw Harden getting into a sleek black Jaguar. I thought I would follow him. Tailing a Jaguar in a huge van wasn't going to be easy, but it was nice that I could see over traffic to watch where he goes.

He drove out Charleston Boulevard towards Maryland and pulled into the Lansome Agency parking lot. Interesting, I thought. What would he be doing here? I pulled in far enough away and watched him get out and go into the building. I wasn't sure if he would remember me, so I decided to follow. I got out and went in the front entrance and stopped at the receptionist desk.

"Hi, I thought I saw Matthew Harden come in here, was I mistaken?" I asked the girl behind the desk.

"No, you were right. He just came in to see Mrs. Lansome."

"Aren't they competitors? Both being agents?"

"They all have interests in the models and sometimes loan one to another agent for a job. Mrs. Lansome was offering to put Amanda Dawson in Vogue, Mr. Harden wouldn't pass a chance like that."

The girl was too chatty for talking to a stranger. But it was good for me. "Well, Vogue, that's good. Who gets the commission for the photo shoot?"

"They split it, that's how they work. Are you in the business?"

"No, I'm investigating the murder of the three models in the competition," I said without saying whether I was police or not.

She made a face, "That was so tragic, do you know who may have done this?"

"We have a few leads. How many of the Lansome models are still in the show?"

"Only one now, Tiffy was the other, but as you know she's dead."

"Yes, she is, tragic. Well, thank you for the information." I started to leave when she asked if I wanted to see Harden. "No, I was just curious why he was here. Thank you again."

"You're welcome. I hope you catch the killer," she replied, and then I went out the door to my van.

A few minutes later, Harden came out of Lansome's office and the receptionist saw him. "Oh, Mr. Harden, you just missed someone asking about you."

He paused, gave her a strange look and asked "Who?"

"I didn't get his name, but he was a policeman. He just wanted to know if it was you. That's all, he left."

Harden went out the front door quickly and stood at the edge of the parking lot looking around. I was still in my van, far enough away where he couldn't really see me. Of course, I was slouching down, which helped. He stood about a minute, then went to his car and drove out. I started my van and drove back to my office.

I came in through the front entrance and saw Lacey, she was back at her desk after taking a long break. "Any word from Earl or Trapper?"

"Nope, guess they don't want to talk to you. Penny's in your office, we've decided to redecorate it."

That had me worried and I rushed in to see what she was up to. The light of my life was at my desk with Willy, doing something on my computer. I came around as she smiled and found her playing solitaire.

"I'm glad you're not plotting something. Lacey said you two were going to redecorate my office."

"She did? That's an interesting idea though." she said looking around the room, "I can see you'd need a woman's touch in here, since you get so many women clients. They'd feel comfortable if I did a little tweaking."

"Yeah, well go tweak the lounge room. The guards would appreciate that. Now may I have my chair back?"

She stood, giving me a kiss on her way up. "Want to fool around?" she teased.

"No, I need to call Lynn. Thank you for the offer and I'll take you up on that later."

"You wish, offer is good only until close of today's business."

"Oh well, I'll just have to make do then, alone." I sat and picked up my desk phone. I could use my cell phone, but I'm paying a fortune for the office phone system, so may as well take advantage of it. I dialed Lynn and she came on.

"Jim, I was just going to call you. Deacon got a lead on Mossa Lefler. You interested in tagging along?"

I looked to Penny; she was walking around my office as though she were sizing it up. "I'm afraid to leave my office, but that sounds good. Should I meet you there?"

"We have a few details to work out here, so come on in."

"May I bring Penny?" I said and she turned to me and shook her head no. "Never mind, she's not wanting to follow us boring people. I'll see you shortly." I hung up and asked her, "Don't want to follow me into the danger zone?"

"Not that, I have an appointment to have my body sculpted."

I gave her a puzzled look and she laughed. "I got an offer to go to a spa and get a make-over."

"What's wrong with your body now?"

"Nothing, I just like to be pampered now and then. Missy Ponser, from Ponser Spa was on my show today and invited me. So I'm going to get the full treatment."

"Well, don't go changing too much," I paused, then said, "Well, if they can sculpt you into looking like Pamela Anderson, I wouldn't object."

She gave me an evil look, walked to my door and went out. I looked to Willy still sitting on my desk and said, "That's going to bite me later." I picked him up and went out to the lobby.

Penny must have went out the back, she wasn't there. "Did Penny go through here?" I asked Lacey.

"No, she went out the back to her car. I watched her on the security camera."

"Thanks, watch Willy, please. I have to go interrogate a criminal."

"Is he the one who murdered the models?"

"We'll find out, I'll let you know," I said and went out the front door to my van. I paused in the outer lobby at Tracey's desk and said, "You need some time in the office. Does Lacey give you any work?"

"Oh yes, she does. She has filing for me to do in the afternoon, so I get to go in."

"Good I don't want to have you become a hermit out here. I"ll be back later, don't get too bored."

"I won't. I'm reading your latest book," she said with a big grin.

"Now that's boring," I laughed and went out.

I arrived at Lynn's office and she was on the phone. Deacon acknowledged me and I sat.

"What's up?" I asked.

"Lynn is talking to Frank Felton, in Vice. He knows about this Mossa Lefler, and Lynn wants the skinny on him before we go."

"You know where he's at?"

"We have a lead, some bar he has an interest in, over on Jones Boulevard by Desert Inn. He's been on Vice's radar for a while. Extortion and illegal gambling."

"A wannabe mob capo?"

Deacon laughed and said, "Yeah, something like that. He's not part of any family, but he has a small crew he keeps around. I guess he is his own mini-mob."

"Maybe I can ask Angelo to inquire, he may be of help to Vice."

"I'm sure he would, I'll talk to the Captain in Vice."

Lynn hung up and smiled. "So shall we go rattle some hoods?"

"Did you get all the dirty details on this guy?"

"Yep, let's go." We went to our cars and drove to the bar. It wasn't much of a place and advertised that it had strippers in the evening. We went in and Lynn asked the bartender, "Is Mossa Lefler in."

"You should know he's not, he was shot over off the strip. Don't you cops inform each other when there is a crime?"

*

Chapter 13

Outside the bar, Lynn pulled her cell phone and called dispatch. She identified herself and asked about a shooting involving a man named Lefler.

"Yes, Lieutenant, there was a shooting involving that person. He was shot about an hour ago, behind Harrah's Hotel, off Koval. He was found by a dumpster, he's in critical condition."

85

"Nothing on the perp?"

"Nothing ma'am, that I know. You can talk to the primary, he may know."

"Who took lead?"

"Detective Walt Lewis, ma'am."

"Thank you, and I don't like being called ma'am," Lynn growled and hung up.

"Careful dear, you'll get a reputation for being mean," Deacon said.

"I'm having hormonal disturbances, leave me alone!" she barked back.

Deacon walked over to where I was, leaving Lynn stomping to her car. "Are you coming or not!" she yelled to Deacon.

"I'll follow you!" I yelled from the safe distance, as Deacon ran to keep up. I went to my van and drove out behind them.

We arrived on Koval Avenue, just off the back of Harrah's Hotel and saw a few black-and-whites parked by a couple of dumpsters for the apartment buildings there. The CSI SUV's were parked up close and I pulled off to the side. Lynn went up to the lead of the CSI, as Deacon followed carefully behind her.

I came up to hear the CSI saying, "Yeah, Detective Lewis just left and the victim was taken by the MedTechs to LV Medical about ten minutes ago. We're just finishing up here."

"What's the prelim?"

"The victim was standing about here," he pointed, "and the bullet came from low. I'd say from a car. It could be just a drive-by, but I'd say the victim knew the perp. He just stood here and took one near the heart. He may live or not, time will tell. A few people who live in the apartments heard the shots and called it in, there was a patrol car here shortly after."

"Okay, I'll talk to Lewis to get his take on it. I think it connects to my case of the murdered models."

"Really? Such a shame, a waste of beautiful women."

"Yea, well, have a little sympathy for the not so beautiful women who are murdered around this stinking town," she grumbled and stormed off.

The CSI looked puzzled and Deacon just said, "Hormones." We followed Lynn as she was standing by her car. She had a pained look on her face.

"What's wrong? Are you okay?" Deacon asked.

She turned to him and started to cry lightly. ""I'm sorry, this whole pregnancy is messing with my system. I'm going back to my office to hide. You go talk to Lewis and see what you can find. Jim can drive you." She got into her car and drove off.

We stood there waiting until she was out of sight. "I'm on pins and needles with her lately. I'll be glad when this pregnancy thing is over."

"Well, you don't have to carry the baby for nine months like she does, then go through the birthing process. I've been there once, with my son, not pleasant. Shall we go track down Lewis?"

"I'll call and see where he's at," he said as he pulled his cell phone. He made a call, finding out his present location, and told the Detective we'd meet him where he was at. Deacon hung up and said, "He's

Lipstick Murders

at the Carl's Jr. over on Maryland. Not a bad time to get something to eat also."

I agreed and we got into the van and drove over. We found Lewis with his partner, George Nerone, sitting at a table, eating their food. They pulled their food trays over as we sat next to them.

"Walt, how's it going?" Deacon asked.

"Good, how's the wife dealing with being pregnant?"

"Don't ask, she's like a bear that just woke from hibernation. What's the scoop on the shooting of Mossa Lefler?"

"I think it was a dispute between him and one of his associates. No witnesses, no shell casing, although it took only one shot, close up. So Lefler had to have known the perp."

"So no one saw the car?"

"Nope, nothing to go on. If some busy body hadn't called it in from the gun shot sound, he might have laid there until someone took out their trash."

"Did Lefler have a car?"

"We looked, but couldn't find one. He may have come along with the perp and after getting out, he took it in the chest. We won't know unless Lefler pulls out of it. What's your interest in this hood?"

"We believe he may have a connection to the Lipstick Killer. Or he could be the Lipstick Killer. We think he or an associate may have been hired to do the job."

"Really? That's not good. Lefler has a history of possible shootings, but never convicted. Who do you think might have hired him?"

88

"One of the agents for the models. We're going to be watching him closely now. This shooting doesn't help."

"Could your agent have shot Lefler?"

I spoke now, "He couldn't have, I was watching him around the time Lefler was shot. He was way up on Charleston and Maryland."

"Do you know anyone called Weasel AKA Darryl?"

"Weasel, yeah, he was an associate of Lefler, why you ask?"

"We understand he may also be the killer. What do you know about him?"

"He's called Weasel because he is. Not very bright, but sneaky. I don't think he's good with a gun, his weapon of choice is a knife. He's kept himself out of trouble, just barely. I doubt he might have shot the women."

"Any idea if Lefler was a good shot?"

"Sure, he was a combat grunt in Iraq. I heard say he could kill a man from a mile away with a good sniper rifle."

Deacon looked to me and smiled. "If you hear anything more, let me know," he said to Lewis.

"Sure, if he comes around, I'll beat him into a comma if he doesn't talk," he said with a wide grin.

Deacon and I went up to order some food as Walt and his partner were leaving. "I'm thinking this is all too easy. We sure got all this good information without breaking a sweat," I said.

"Yeah, but it seems to fit. Harden wants his girl to win the big prize, so he hires Lefler to take out the money babes and then Harden has Lefler taken out to cover his tracks."

"So will Harden have to hire someone to take out the second killer, and so on? This could get complicated."

"And it doesn't help when you bring things like that up. It makes my job all that much harder," Deacon moaned.

"Why? Because you have to think? You must have really enjoyed being in Vice, no investigating, just straight out arresting the hookers and pimps," I said with a smirk.

"There's more to Vice than that. I have to think while working there too. Can we just get on with this?"

"Sure, so where do we go from here?" I asked.

"What? You expect me to think? I'll just follow your lead for a while and see where that takes us." Now he was smirking.

We got into the van and I sat there thinking. "Okay, what have we got so far? Three dead models, one overzealous agent and a near dead criminal. I'd say the case is going well."

"You got nothing," Deacon grinned.

"We could go question Mrs. Lansome," I said. "She had a meeting with Harden around the time Lefler was hit. Maybe she can help us."

"You have to start the van first."

"You want to explain next how to drive?" I said. Deacon laughed, as I started the van and drove over to the Lansome Agency.

We went in the front entrance and the same woman, from when I was there earlier, was at the reception desk. "Hey, you're that cop asking about Mr. Harden, aren't you?" she bubbled as we came up.

"I asked about Harden, but I never said I was a cop. I said I was investigating the murders, I'm a private investigator. Now this gentleman is cop," I said pointing to Deacon.

He moved forward and spoke, "I'm Detective D'Angelo, may we see Mrs. Lansome?"

"I'll see if see's taking appointments," the woman said.

"I'm not asking for an appointment, tell her if she won't see us, she can be taken into police H.Q. and be questioned there." Deacon gave her a big smile and she picked up the phone explaining the situation. She listened and then hung up. "Mrs. Lansome will see you shortly. Please wait here."

I whispered to Deacon, "She's playing the control card. You can wait for me, Officer."

The door to Lansome's office opened and a young, slinky, red-headed woman walked out. She smiled at us and said, "Officers, you can go in now."

Deacon grinned and thanked her. We went into the office. I closed the door behind me as Deacon went to her desk. He flashed his badge and said, "I don't know if you remember me from the other day, as you were rushing away. I'm Detective D'Angelo. This gentleman is Jim Richards, a consultant to LVMPD. We're still investigating the murder of your model. I hope you'll cooperate."

"Detective, I am appalled by the murder of Tiffy. I'll do whatever you need to catch this killer. Tiffy had a bright future and she would have, excuse me for being blunt, made this agency a lot of money."

"What can you tell me about Matthew Harden?"

"I wouldn't trust him with my life. He's an asshole," she said without blinking.

*

Chapter 14

I was a bit surprised by this woman's answer. She didn't seem like the kind of lady who would think this way, but then again, Harden did seem to be an asshole.

"Could you elaborate on your opinion?" Deacon asked.

"He's a sharp, shrewd man, but he can't be trusted. He would steal a client model if you turn your back on him. I try to stay cordial with him in my dealings, but I have to watch him closely."

"He was in here earlier, what was that about?"

"I had a request for an extra model to do a photo shoot for Vogue, and since my best model, Tiffy, was murdered, I asked Matthew if I could use one of his models. Amanda Dawson, in particular, she's the top model now with the others gone."

"Did he agree to the loan of his model?"

"Of course, getting in Vogue is a feather in the cap of a model. And more money for her agent. She is worth millions over her lifetime… if she lives."

I thought the way she said that was peculiar, like she had an agenda also. "Do you have any models in the competition now who could win?" I asked.

"My girls are all good, but unless Amanda screws up badly, she'll probably take the crown. I wouldn't put it past Matthew to have had a hand in the deaths. You really should keep an eye on him."

"Thank you, Mrs. Lansome, We intend to do that. We'll let you get back to your business, thank you again." He put his business card on her desk.

Deacon nodded to me and then turned to go out, he stopped at the door and asked, "If you hear anything, call me." He turned and went out.

Outside the building I asked, "What's your feelings on that woman?"

"I think she's ruthless, but I don't see why she would murder her own women to let Harden's girl win. Doesn't make sense."

"I agree, but there's something off about her. Shouldn't we go interrogate the models?" I said.

"You'd love that, wouldn't you? I'm so telling Penny."

"You've been a lot meaner since Lynn started being a pregnant woman."

"Hey, I get it from her, I give it to you," he said with an evil laugh and walked to my van, I followed.

Once seated in the vehicle, I asked, "So where do we find the models?"

Lipstick Murders

"Let's go back to the Mall, they're still running the fashion show, with added security."

"You got it, grumpy."

"I'm hardly a dwarf," he said.

"Well, you're not Happy, Sleepy, Doc, Sneezy or Bashful. But you could be Dopey."

"Just shut up and drive," he mumbled. I tried not to laugh out loud, and drove out.

We arrived at the Fashion Show Mall and parked back by the trailers again. We went to the make-up trailer and went in. Mr. David was still prancing around getting the models made up and saw Deacon. He shrieked softly and came to us.

"Detective D'Angelo, how good to see you again," he bubbled.

I was waiting for him to give Deacon a kiss. I wasn't going to laugh.

"Mr. David, we need to talk to Amanda Dawson. Is she here?"

"Yes, she is. If you can get past her security men. All big and viral they are," he grinned.

I wonder if Buck had supplied the extra guards. I'd have to ask him later.

Mr. David yelled for Amanda, shortly she came over followed by four big men in deep purple blazers embroidered with the 'Richards Investigation and Security Agency' on the pocket. Now I knew. One of the men recognized me and acknowledged me.

"Mr. Richards, good to see you on the job," the big man said.

"Thanks, Ralph," I replied. He told the other men to go take a break and left us alone with the model. I could see why she would be a contender for the win. She was beautiful and had a grace about her. Besides, she was a sexy little thing.

"Miss Dawson, I'm Detective D'Angelo and this is Jim Richards. We need to talk."

"Sure, I just finished, so I can talk. Is this about Tiffy?"

"That's part of it, there were two others murdered. Aren't you afraid for your life?"

"Of course I am. I'm no fool. My agent, Matthew Harden, is concerned about my safety. So I'm comfortable with the arrangements he set up with these guards. Now what do you want to know?"

"Would you have any thoughts on the murders of these models?" Deacon asked.

"I have no idea why. I assume there was someone who had a vendetta against them. They most likely made enemies in their journey to the spotlight."

"With the three of them gone, you have a better chance of winning now."

"I certainly hope you're not insinuating that I had anything to do with their murders. I can stand up to any model on the runway and keep my head up. Don't even say I had anything to do with this. I could win on my own, even if Tiffy was still in the competition."

"I'm not accusing, it's just a question to eliminate you from the suspects. I presume you were at Harden's celebration party the night Tiffy was murdered?"

"I was, with a dozen people around me. I have an alibi."

"As I figured. What is your opinion of Matthew Harden? As an agent and as a person?"

"He's a strange man, but he does the job. He keeps me working, and I get paid well. But then, so does he. I guess that's what it's all about, the money."

"Didn't you get into the business because you wanted to be a model?" I asked.

She looked to me as if she forgot I was there. "I didn't at first. Matthew picked me out of a local talent contest, where I was singing. He pushed me to being his client and I said I would. He made me what I am, the next top model."

I thought, yeah, helped by a couple dead bodies. "Would you say Matthew would stoop to murder to make sure you would be the winner of the competition?" I asked.

Now she looked at me like I was a bug. "Now you are saying that Matthew murdered those women? What is wrong with you people? We are honest and hardworking. We don't need to murder the competition, we do our best and we win." She stood, "I'm sorry, but I'm done for now. I have to go." She stormed out of the trailer and disappeared.

"Well, I'd say you hit a sour note with her," Deacon said with a grin.

"Some people are just too sensitive when it comes to murder."

"Okay, since we are here, shall we question a few others?"

"I won't object," I replied.

"Of course you won't," Deacon grinned and walked over to a table where a rather young looking brunette was seated, looking into a mirror. "Excuse me," Deacon said, as he flashed his shield. "May we ask you a couple questions?"

She looked at his badge and said, "Cops, eh? What do you want?"

"First, what's your name."

"Mandy Barker."

"Well, Mandy, I'd like your take on the murders this last week."

"Sure, be glad to help, Amanda Dawson did it."

That quick statement took both of us by surprise. Deacon asked, "Why do you say that?"

"She's a bitch, and she wants to win. She'll do anything to get ahead of the rest of us. I know she's the next in line to win, that's why she disposed of the competition. With Tiffy and the others out of the way, she's a shoe in."

"You evidently don't think you'll win?" I asked.

"It's like American Idol, the runners up get airtime on national TV and get exposure. They also get picked up by recording companies to put out records. Even if they didn't win. I may not get the top prize in this stupid contest, but I will be seen my millions, and a good number of agents who can do me good."

"Who's your agent now?"

"Annabelle Meyer, she's just temporary though, so I could get in the competition."

Lipstick Murders

"Temporary? You don't plan to stay with her?"

"Depends on how I do in the contest. Even Amanda is scouting around for a new agent, but don't tell Harden that. He's a bastard and probably would strangle her, if he knew."

I looked to Deacon and said quietly, "Well, that puts a new light on the matter. If Harden knew, would he have murdered the women?"

"I'm assuming he doesn't know." He turned back to the woman, "Do you believe Harden is capable of murder?"

"Listen doll-face, all agents would murder to get their piece of beef in the spotlight. I work independently, but it's part of the rules that I needed an agent to get into this sideshow. That's why I got Annabelle to sponsor me. She knows the game, and helped me. As for Harden, I'm sure he wouldn't murder anyone, he's a wimp. But he sure would hire someone to do the job."

I figured Deacon was satisfied by her answers, he said, "Thank you for your help, it's appreciated." He turned and led me out of the trailer. "I'm getting some vibes on this. We pretty much know Harden did it, but how to prove it."

"Maybe we need to talk to Amanda again to get her take on dumping Harden," I said.

"True. Maybe she'll be more receptive, if we let her know that we know."

*

Chapter 15

Deacon called to Mr. David, when he saw him standing outside the make-up trailer. "Excuse me," he said as we approached him.

"Well, it's the big, strong police officer. How nice. What can I do for you?" he smiled at Deacon, as the big guy blushed.

"Uh, can you tell me where Amanda Dawson went?" he stuttered.

"Amanda? Oh, you swing in her direction? How sad. I saw her go into the wardrobe trailer, trying on gowns, I guess." He pointed to a large trailer and then went off.

We walked over to the trailer and came up to the four bodyguards again. Ralph smiled and let us pass. We entered the trailer, as there was a flurry of women running around with clothing flying right and left. In the middle of the storm, we saw Amanda sitting quietly in the middle of the madness.

Deacon went to her and she gave him a frown. "You shouldn't frown, Amanda, it will cause wrinkles."

"So, Mr. Cop is an expert on women's problems," she snarled.

"My wife, a homicide Lieutenant, is pregnant, I know a little about women's problems. We need to talk to you, in private."

"I'm done talking to police. Go away."

Lipstick Murders

"Amanda, we can talk here, or I'll have you hauled into LVMPD to be questioned there. Your choice?"

She sat mulling that over and said, "Okay. What do you want?"

"We should talk privately. Unless you don't mind everyone hearing that you wanted to dump Harden as your agent."

She gave Deacon a look that suggested she was willing to talk in private. "Where do you want to go? This place has people everywhere."

I whispered to Deacon that we could use my motorhome van, it was private. He smiled and asked Amanda to follow us. The three of us left the trailer, followed by her entourage of hulking body guards. I asked them to wait outside the van, as Deacon led her in. We walked to the back of the van, where the dining table was set up instead of the bed. We sat on the side benches around the temporary table set up for meals or enjoying company.

"Amanda, we have word that you were planning on firing Matthew Harden as your manager. Talk to me."

She sat chewing on her inside cheek. She was looking around the motorhome and said, "This is nice, it's like a little home. Does it have a bathroom?"

"Yes, it does, and a kitchen and bedroom, if you move a few things around," I replied, then continued, "Now, what about Harden?"

She sat back on the bench and looked out the back window of the van. "I was planning on dumping Matthew after the competition. He's a jerk and was only thinking about the money he can make off me. He never really cared about me as a person," She paused and was doing some thinking. She finally came out of her trance and said, "When we first met, at the Miss Silverdust Beauty Pageant, he was all enthusiastic about wanting me as a client for modeling. At first, I figured he was some creep wanting me for sex. I took his card and then asked around, it turned out he was legit. Most of the girls I talked to said he was a bit odd, but he was a real agent. I was thrilled and contacted him to see what he could do for me. He started me out with small jobs, to get my feet wet, as he said." She looked around, "Does this place have water? My throat is dry."

"Would you like some soda pop? Diet, I presume?" I asked.

"Yes, that would be nice, soda water, if you have it."

I stood and walked to the small refrigerator, and took out a can of Diet Sprite that I usually had on hand for Buck. I gave it to her after I popped the top. She thanked me and sat thinking again. "Everything I tell you is not going back to Matthew?"

"No, unless you tell us, it's all right," Deacon said.

"Matthew did try to get me into bed with him twice, we were both drunk, but I wasn't stupid. I turned him down, he wasn't happy. But what could he say, my contract had clauses that could break our agreement and get me out of it. I made sure that pandering by him was included, so I could get out from under his thumb. I wasn't going to give him any

101

leeway to seduce me." She paused to take a drink from the can, and then was quiet for a bit. We didn't push.

"Are all contracts the same for model agent relationships?" I asked.

"Oh, hell no. Every agency has different contracts. I had a lawyer look over mine before I signed and made it specific about my feelings." She paused again, another sip of pop. "Can I be honest here? You can't tell anyone what I'm about to say?"

"We won't, we just need the truth." Deacon said.

"I don't want anyone to know this yet, until I'm ready to come out." She stopped and looked out the back window again. It was facing the trailers where the models were still running around. She looked back to us and said, "I'm a lesbian." She took a sip again.

"Do you feel this will hurt your modeling career, if it got out?" I asked.

"Not really, but the tabloids would have a field day with it," she said sadly.

"Actually, I think it's a bit hot. A sexy model and a lesbian," Deacon said.

She stared at him a minute, enough to make him uncomfortable. "Men all think alike. It's sexy for two women to be together, especially models. I don't like the way I was born. I hid it for years, but it's getting harder, especially when I'm around beautiful women in slinky clothing. It's even harder to watch them dress and undress for these shows. I don't think they'd like it either, if they knew. Models are odd people. So I have been in hiding. Tiffy was a lesbian, too."

That statement caught both Deacon and I by surprise. "How did you know this?" I asked.

"We just have a way of telling. One night when Tiffy and I were alone after a photo shoot, I confronted her. She didn't admit it at first, I confessed to her I was, then she admitted her feelings. We had a very brief and causal affair. It didn't last; she was too wrapped up in her career to be hooked up in a scandal with me. I didn't need it either, so we made an agreement to be quiet about it. I was devastated when I heard she was murdered. I had words with Matthew about her death. I felt he may have had something to do with it. He was a bastard enough to pull something like that."

I remembered Harden's assistant, Betsy, telling us about overhearing that heated discussion, which is what led us to Harden. Deacon gave me a nod of acknowledgement, too.

"Do you think Harden could have set up the murders of all three women?" Deacon asked.

She had a blank stare and then said, "As much as I hope I'm wrong, I think he did have something to do with it. Those poor women, they didn't deserve to die so I could win this stupid contest."

"Why don't you drop out and see what he does?" I asked.

"Are you crazy? He's invested so much into this, he would probably kill me," she said with a shocked look.

I had a thought and I asked Deacon to follow me up front of the van. "We'll be right back, Amanda."

Lipstick Murders

I stopped by the front seats and turned to Deacon. "We should set her up to confront Harden about her wanting to quit the show. I think this would be a good idea to draw out Harden to see what he would do if she tried to drop out."

"Jim that could be dangerous for her. If Harden did arrange to kill the others, he could do the same for her."

"I don't think so. As she said, he has a lot invested in her. But if she just suggests it, he may do something or say something that would incriminate him. We could have her wired when she tells him, and see where it goes."

He mulled it over in his head then said, "It could work. We'd have her watched and could protect her. Let's throw it at her and see."

We went back to the table and I spoke, "Amanda, we believe that Matthew had a hand in the murder of the women. We could be wrong, but we need some proof that he did or didn't. Detective D'Angelo and I have a plan if you are agreeable. We would put a wire on you, then you would go to him and tell him you want out of the competition. Just to see what he says or does. With the wire, we would be with you the entire time, if he gets violent. I don't think he will. We just want to see what he says or does. If he's clean, you can tell him you'll go through with it. That should keep him happy and leave you alone. If he's dirty, we can arrest him and you'd be out of his contract."

"We'd be watching you the whole time. You'd be protected," Deacon said, hopefully to calm her.

"Do you really think this would work?" she asked.

"We won't know until we try. But only if you are agreeable."

"I want justice for Tiffy, I did have a bit of love for her," she paused again, then said, "Okay, let's see what happens. I'm agreeable."

*

Chapter 16

Deacon was happy that she was going to cooperate. I could tell, he usually had this special look when he was happy or just had sex. Not that I would know the sex look first hand. He turned to me and said, "We need to set this up with Lynn." Then he looked to Amanda, "Just go through your normal everyday activities, we have to get this set up. I'll call you when we have everything arraigned. Just play along with Harden and be cool."

"I have endured him this long, I guess I can for a while longer," she replied.

"I'll need your cell number so I can reach you."

She opened her tiny purse and pulled out a business card, handed it to Deacon and stood. "May I go now? I have to do some business."

"I'm done, thank you. I'll be in touch," Deacon said as I stood and walked her to the door of the van. She bounced off as Deacon came up behind me. We left the van and stood watching the models scurrying around.

"Well, we may have something to go on yet," Deacon said with a smile.

"Shall we retreat to the precinct?" I asked. He agreed and we got back into the van and I drove to the LVMPD.

We found Lynn and Penny in the break room, having snacks and coffee. We sat as Deacon explained our meeting with Amanda.

"So we may be able to get him to screw up and admit to this?" Lynn asked.

"That's the plan. Hopefully, he'll be nuts enough to shoot off his mouth. We need a wire on her, can you arrange that?" Deacon asked.

She squinted at him for a bit too long. Deacon cringed, and said, "Of course you can, you are the Lieutenant after all."

"Thank you," she said, with a little ice in her voice. She sat looking around the room at the people laughing and eating. "I'm sorry. I guess this pregnancy is turning me into a real bitch. Please be patient with me."

Deacon took her hand and held it tightly. "Honey, I understand. I can take as much abuse as you can dish out. Just don't let the baby be as mean."

Everyone laughed, and Lynn finally broke a smile. "Okay, I'll get the electronics lab on the wire. You'll need to have her come in. Think that will be a problem?"

"I don't think so, she seemed to want to get out of her contract with Harden, so this could help her."

"I'll call Larry and have him arrange it. See about getting her in here."

"I'll have Greg Warren go pick her up on the Q.T. and we can set her up," Deacon said.

"Sounds like a plan. You are now in charge of this sting, I'm taking a little down time and go shopping with Penny. I'll see you back home later."

Lynn stood and led Penny out of the break room, after Penny gave me a kiss. She whispered in my ear, "Don't worry, I won't spend too much."

I cringed and told her to be careful. I looked to Deacon, "Well, it's up to you big guy."

"What? You aren't deserting me now are you?"

"No, I'm still in this. Until I get tired of all the sexy women we have to watch," I said with a smirk.

"Okay, let's go take care of business." Deacon smiled and stood.

~~*~~

Buck was sitting at the table next to the stage watching Laynie Keller, singing a slow sexy tune to the large crowd that turned out for her opening afternoon matinee show. The Silver Slipper lounge was huge and accommodated about 250 people, all sitting at tables, eating or drinking. There was a fairly ample dance floor in front of the stage for couples to mingle when the dance band played. Right now the dance floor was empty, as Laynie performed her tunes from her latest album.

Buck was entranced by her beauty, but realized he had to be on his toes to protect her. He had seen the messages sent by the stalker and knew this was a sick individual. The stalker had described in detail how he was going to treat Laynie when he got her to himself. He was not kind and it was just downright sick. Buck wasn't going to let that happen.

He glanced around the room and spotted the two men from his security guard team, standing in the back of the room scanning the crowd for any activity. He decided it was better to add a couple strong arms to help watch. Not that he didn't think he could handle it, but things get a bit crazy in most cases, and a few good extra men would be a big help.

Laynie stepped down from the stage, with her wireless microphone, and went across the dance floor to the front table where a couple sat looking so in love. Laynie sang a love song for them and then when she finished, she came over to Buck. He shrunk from the attention and the spotlight, as she sat on his lap and sang a bawdy song in his ear. Everyone laughed at the sight of this huge man turning red.

Laynie kissed the top of his bald head and stood as she finished. "Ladies and gentlemen, this is my protector, Buck Carson. Don't even mess with him, he's dangerous." Everyone applauded as Buck just sat there taking the friendly abuse.

A voice rang out from the audience, "He doesn't look so tough. Laynie, I'll make you mine soon."

Buck was trying to pinpoint from where the voice came from. His men moved forward to seek out the person, but they couldn't spot him.

Laynie looked a little spooked, "Well, that's from a fan I don't need. I'm not into relationships, but thank you." She went back up on the stage and had her small band play an upbeat tune. She turned and told everyone to get up and dance. They did.

Buck was moving over to see the stage better as the people started to dance in front of him. He signaled to his men to move closer and they did. Buck was at the side foot of the stage when he saw an arm reach out to Laynie and grab her wrist. Buck sprang across the stage and tackled the man, both of them falling to the ground on the dance floor. People were moving away, as Buck wrestled the man into an arm lock. Buck's men came rushing up and grabbed on to the struggling attacker. Buck brought out his cuffs and secured the man as they hustled him out of the room. Buck stayed back to watch Laynie, just in case.

"Well folks," Laynie said into the mic, "I told you don't mess with my protector."

Everyone applauded and Buck took a quick bow and then led Laynie through the back curtain to the backstage area. She was shaking really bad and Buck put his arms around her to settle her.

"It's over. He's going to be taken by the police, as soon as they get here. My men will see to it. Just take a deep breath and relax."

She looked up to him and said, "I have to finish the set. The audience is waiting."

He lead her back to the opening and she went out to applause. "Thank you everyone. Now we had a little excitement, but I have more show for you. So let's get on with it." She told her band leader to give her one of her famous pop songs. Buck was watching again from the side. He didn't trust anything to seem like it was over.

He pulled his cell phone and called one of the men who had the attacker. "John, what's happening?"

The man replied, "Hotel security has him now and they are waiting for the police. He's yelling that he just wanted to hold her hand, not to harm her. But he'll be questioned."

"There are security cameras aimed at the stage, mention it to the police. Maybe it will show a different motive for his grab." He hung up and stood silently watching Laynie perform.

~~*~~

Detective Greg Warren brought Amanda Dawson through the back of the police building, to keep her from being seen. Not that Harden would be watching, but it didn't hurt to be cautious.

He led her to the squad room where Deacon had arranged for Larry to wire her. She was looking a bit frightened by it all. I moved over to her and put my arm around her shoulder.

"Amanda, you have nothing to be worried about. This is all good, and this way we will find out what Harden is up to. Just relax, and it will be all over before you know it."

She smiled at me, but it was a weak smile. I took her to a chair as Deacon sat before her.

"Larry here is from our electronics lab, and will put a wireless mic on you so we can hear everything that is being said. Do you understand?"

"Yeah, I do watch cop shows on TV. Unfortunately, most people with the wire get caught and killed," she said meekly.

"That's TV, Amanda. In real life people never get killed with a wire. We will be watching for you. If he tries anything, we will close in and stop him. Okay?"

"Let's do this, then. I want to get it over and done with. What do I have to do?"

Larry stepped up and said, "I have a woman officer who will wire you in that room over there." He pointed. "It's private so no one will see you."

A female cop came over and led her to the room, as I went up to Deacon.

"Is that true that no one has ever been killed because of a wire?" I asked.

He looked up to me from the chair. "Okay, so I made it up. Hardly anyone gets killed."

*

Chapter 17

"You know you're going to hell for lying," I laughed.

"Hey, lying is part of the job, or we'd never get the cases solved. Now, how are we going to use her?"

"Send her to Harden saying she's too frightened to continue, she doesn't want to be the next victim. He'll have to reassure her that she won't be murdered. Only the real killer would know this. Have her really push him hard to get verification that she'll be safe. He'll have to say something."

"Yeah, it could work. He seems to be a bull head and shoots his mouth off. If she's backing out, he'll do what he can to keep her in. I just hope Amanda is smart enough to push his right buttons," Deacon turned as the door to the office opened and Amanda came out.

"This thing is annoying," she moaned.

"You'll only have to wear it to talk to him, just tell him you want out because you're afraid for your life. He'll try and talk you out of it. You'll push about how he could know you'll be safe. Work it around him admitting to anything about the killings. All we need is him to admit to the murders of Tiffy and the others and we'll move in. If he still refuses to admit it, just play along and get out."

"I always wanted to act, so this is my big chance. I'll give you an Oscar performance," she said with too much bravado.

"Just play your role as a model afraid for her life. Don't overdo it, or he may get suspicious. As I said, we'll be listening. Shall we go to his office?"

She hesitated, but then said, "I'll do my best."

Larry packed up his equipment and said he'd have the surveillance van ready to go. Deacon had Greg Warren drive her back to the modeling agency as I took Deacon in my van. We followed Greg to Harden's office and parked. Deacon got out and went to the surveillance van as I followed.

Greg had dropped her off just down from the entrance so she wouldn't be seen getting out of his car. He pulled out and parked in the next lot over. He was on his radio, in case he was needed.

We listened on the headphones as she went in to the building and back towards Harden's private office. She asked the receptionist if she could talk to Matthew.

"Sure, Amanda. He's not busy right now. I'll call him." She picked up her phone and called him. After a moment of conversation, she hung up. "He said to go right in."

"Thanks," Amanda said and went to the door. She stopped just before opening it, she stood thinking.

"I hope she's not having second thoughts," Deacon said, when we heard her pause. Then we heard her turn the door knob and open the door. We could hear Harden call to her.

"Amanda, how are you today. All ready for the big night?" he said with taking a pause.

"Matthew… I need to talk to you about that," she spoke with a slight shake to her voice.

"What's the matter babe, you're not worrying about winning are you? Don't even think about it, you are a shoo-in," he said standing, and coming around his desk to her. We could hear his voice closer now.

"Matthew, it's not the winning I'm concerned about. It's the murders. You know that there was a warning written on Tiffy's wall about more killings. Two more girls died since then. I'm not putting myself out for getting killed."

"Amanda, doll, you'll be alright. Hey, where are your goons? Shouldn't you have your bodyguards?"

"Crap," Deacon muttered, "We forgot about her guards."

We heard Amanda pause again, "Uh, I had them go get some food, they've watched me all day and they needed to eat."

"Good save," I said. "Deacon, I'll call Buck and get his men back to her now." I pulled my phone and called, told Buck what we needed and he said he'd take care of it.

Harden spoke, "Now listen, we will be real careful with you. When your guards get back, they will not leave you alone for a minute."

"Matthew I can't do it. Lana Rule was shot from a long distance. How are my guards going to protect me from that?" Her voice was sounding panicked now, I hope she was acting.

"Amanda, nothing will harm you. I guarantee it."

"Matthew, how the hell can you guarantee anything? Three women have been murdered. I'm not going to be next."

We heard silence for too long. I looked to Deacon, "I hope her mic hasn't malfunctioned." Then we heard him clear his throat.

"Amanda, I believe who ever did this is not going to trouble you."

"How can you know this Matthew? You have some fucking crystal ball? I'm not getting killed for you to make money off me." Her voice was about three octaves higher now, good acting I thought.

"Amanda sit down, I have something to tell you."

Deacon said, "Here it comes."

There was a silence for too long, we waited and could hear movement.

"So talk, Matthew, how do you know I'll be safe?"

Silence again. Then, "I got a call yesterday. Some guy saying he had big money on your winning and he wanted to insure his bet so he… made arrangements for the contest to go your way. I know he won't hurt you, he's got big bucks riding on you. If anything, you are protected."

"Are you saying you knew this guy was murdering the models and you said nothing to the police?" she just about screamed.

"Amanda, take it easy. This is after they were killed, nothing I could do about it. Besides, I knew you were going to be safe. What would it do to bring the police into it?"

"Why did he call you? Why would he tell you this? What good would it do to tell you?" she spoke angrily.

"Amanda, it wouldn't bring back the girls. I had no idea this was happening before they were killed. I would have done something then."

"You know what Matthew, you're a shit! Why don't I believe your bullshit story? Are you covering something? You would have a big interest in my winning, how can I know you didn't have these women murdered?"

"Amanda! I'd never do that. I told you the other day when we spoke, I was fearful for your safety and

Lipstick Murders

I didn't have anything to do with their deaths. I'll swear on a stack of bibles that I didn't."

I looked to Deacon, "I don't think he's going to give it up."

"Doesn't look that way," he said.

There was silence again, then Amanda spoke, more calmer this time. "Okay Matthew, I get it. You are just an innocent agent doing his job. You would never stoop so low as to murder any women to get what you want. I had to know, although I did believe you did this, but you're not going to admit to such a brilliant plan. Smart man."

"She's turning it around now," I said.

"Brilliant plan? Why do you think that?" Matthew said carefully.

"Come on Matthew, it worked didn't it. I'll probably take the win and you'll be a rich man, the big Kahuna of agents. You had it worked out just right didn't you? I almost fell for your sob story about some guy calling you."

"Amanda, I'm not jerking you around. He did call. Are you saying now that you approve of the murders?"

"Hell no, Matthew. I don't approve of the murders, I just want to win. You did a good job to see that happen, didn't you?"

"Amanda, I'm serious, I didn't have anything to do with the murders!" he said, sounding desperate now.

Silence again.

"Okay, I'll leave it at that. If you are lying to me, I'll have your balls."

We could hear movement and then a door open and close. We could hear her mutter under her breath, "Asshole!"

Minutes later, she walked out of the building. Deacon stepped out of the van and whistled to her low. She came over and he helped her in the surveillance van. "Get this damn thing off me, he didn't crack. Worst thing is, I believe that little shit."

"You'd have to remove your blouse to get the wire off you, we can go back and the female cop can help with that," Deacon said.

She suddenly pulled open her blouse, stripped it and yelled, "Get it off me! Now!"

Larry came over to her and carefully pulled the tape holding the equipment on her body. I could see the smirk on his face and he slowly worked to remove the transmitter. We all got a good look.

~~*~~

Buck was talking to the officers who arrived to take the attacker away. Laynie was standing nearby listening.

"I saw him reach out from the front of the stage and grabbed onto her wrist. I jumped over and tackled him, my men then came over and held him till they took him out for you guys to arrive. Also, I'd like my cuffs back, please."

The cop smiled and said he'd get them to Buck. "Miss Keller, we'll need you to file a complaint so we can proceed with this. Is this the stalker you told us about the other day?"

117

"I don't know if it's him, I never saw him, just his calls. But I'll press charges against him if it will help."

Buck smiled and said, "It will help."

*

Chapter 18

Larry had finished removing the wire from Amanda, and she put her blouse back on. "Get an eyeful?" she smiled, "I'm used to dressing and undressing around people because of the shows. Besides, I'm not exposing anything of importance. Now what do we do? He didn't confess."

"We could grab him for withholding the phone call, but as he said it was after the fact. Besides if we take him for that, we'd have to explain that you were wired to trap him. That may not be good for your future," Deacon finished and turned to me. "We need to find out who this voice on the phone was."

"You'd need his phone records, but with a warrant. Unless you told him Amanda came to you concerned for her safety, and told you about the phone call," I said, "Just tell Harden that you're not going to prosecute him for withholding if he gives permission to pull his phone records."

"That could work, but if he refuses, then we're back to the problem of Amanda telling on him," Deacon replied.

Amanda spoke, "Why don't you threaten to shut down the contest for the safety of the rest of the girls, unless he gives you permission to get his records?"

Deacon smiled, "I like the way you think, Amanda. We could do that as an ace in the hole, if he balks. I'm still puzzled why the killer would call him to tell him of the crime."

"I think he, the killer, wanted to be sure that Harden didn't pull Amanda from the contest for her own good. He wanted be sure that Amanda would compete and win," I surmised.

"But, even though I have the lead, what if I didn't win?" Amanda asked.

"I think whoever did the murders would be a little pissed, losing the bet after killing the competition. He might even come after Harden or you to get revenge," I said to Amanda.

"Great, so I'm still dead. I may just go back home to Illinois until this is all over," Amanda said quietly.

I looked to Deacon, "May not be a bad idea if she did just vanish."

Deacon thought a moment, "Yeah, then the killer may call on Harden again to find out why. We could get a tap on his phone. I'll talk to Lynn about this." He turned to Amanda, "Do you think you could just hide out for a few days until the contest?"

"I've got a friend who I could stay with. Do you think it may do any good?"

"We won't know until we try. It could work," he said and looked to me, "Think it might work?"

Lipstick Murders

"Hey, anything is possible, this is worth trying. If there isn't a mysterious caller, then it may tip Harden's hand." I deduced.

"Okay then, I think Amanda should just disappear, with a call to the news saying she's dropping out for her own safety. That would put it out to the public and tip the betting scales. If there is a gambler who bet heavy on Amanda, then he will do what he can to get her back in the competition. Maybe even threaten Harden to get her back. We really need to talk to Lynn."

Deacon picked up the van's radio to call for Warren. "I'll have Detective Warren take you to your place to get some things packed and then to this friend of yours. I'll need a number there," he said to Amanda and then called Warren to drive over.

Deacon gave her last minute details and sent her off with Warren. We stood next to the van and I said. "I hope this works, for her sake. She's invested herself in this contest and she doesn't need to feel threatened."

"Well, it seems that she's actually being protected by unknown suspects who wants to make money off of her. This may make some people very unhappy. Shall we go inform Lynn of your plan?"

"My plan? Why are you giving me all the credit? Oh I see, if it doesn't work you can blame me," I groused.

"Hey, you're not living with an ornery pregnant woman, I am. So suck it up and take the blame, or the honor, if it works. Now let's go get this moving," Deacon smiled and headed to my van.

~~*~~

Buck stood outside the theatre in the back lot watching the uniforms put the suspect in the patrol car. The officer in charge asked him, "Why would he try and do a grab right in front of hundreds of witnesses?"

"I was thinking the same thing. I don't think he's the stalker, just some drunk guy who got a bit too frisky."

"Well, he was crying about not wanting to hurt her, just to dance with her. I think he's straight, but we'll let him settle in the tank overnight, then cut him loose with a stern warning. Unless Miss Keller wants to pursue sterner measures?"

"I'll calm her and see that he gets his ass back in one piece. Thanks for your help," Buck grinned and walked back to Laynie.

"Is he the one?" she asked.

"Honestly, I don't think so. He's just some overzealous drunk who should have left well enough alone. They're tossing him in the drunk tank for the night and see what he says in the morning. They'll determine if he's a threat to you."

"So, my stalker is still out there? Thank you, Buck, for being there for me." She kissed him on the cheek, he blushed, and she giggled.

Buck's guards came up and asked if they were still needed. Buck looked to Laynie and asked. "You're done with this show, when's the next?"

Lipstick Murders

"Tonight, an evening show at seven," She replied.

He turned back to his men, "Go take a break and be back here by six." They agreed and left. Buck led Laynie back in through the stage door and to her dressing room.

She went to her dressing table and pulled off the wig she wore for the show. She started to remove her make-up as Buck asked, "You want me to wait outside while you change?"

"No, you can stay here with me. I change behind that dressing screen," she said pointing to the ornate decorated screen. "It once belonged to a famous performer in vaudeville, I bought it at an auction of her estate. The thing has traveled with me for a number of years when I was gaining more fame." She stood and went behind the screen and talked from there. "Are you a native of Vegas?"

"No, I'm from Michigan. I moved out here a couple years back with my good friend Jim Richards. We started the investigating and security firm together. I run the security, he plays detective."

"Sounds interesting. It must keep you busy. Are you married?"

"Nope, I have a girlfriend, we live together. She's a showgirl at the Tropicana and works most nights. We get along together just fine."

"Oh, too bad, I wouldn't mind getting to know you better," she laughed from behind the screen as clothing flew over it.

Buck was feeling a little heat in his face as she said that. "My girl, Maria, would do serious damage to me if I fooled around. Sorry."

She came around, dressed in street clothing and said, "Lucky man to have such a woman. A showgirl and jealous. Does she know you're guarding me?"

Buck paused a bit too long and she laughed. "Ah, I see. This is business and you don't have to keep her informed on all your cases."

"Something like that. I will tell her eventually, when she's in a good mood," he smiled.

"Bring her to the show, so I can meet her and ease her mind that I won't try and steal you away."

"It's a thought, and I'll have all my friends with her to keep her from hurting me." Now he laughed aloud.

~~*~~

Lynn listened to what we had to say about our afternoon at Hardens. "It sounds like a good plan, you just have to get Harden to cooperate now. He did withhold info about the call. We could hold him on that - impeding an investigation for murder. I'm glad you have it all worked out, I'm in no mood to handle this, other than calls for warrants or a favor or two. So get it started and see where it leads. You have two days before the competition starts, I'm sure Amanda doesn't want to be left out. Talk to the contest official and let them know she will be back."

"What if one of the contest officials is in on the murders?" I asked.

123

Lipstick Murders

"True. Then hold back on that and go with your instincts, just get it rolling." Lynn stood from behind her desk, her protruding belly making it difficult to move. "Why women want children is beyond me. They should have to wear some kind of pillow thing for a couple months just to see how uncomfortable it is." She stopped in front of Deacon and continued, "This is all your fault, but I'll let it go for now." She looked to Penny and asked, "Want to go back out and spend obscene amounts of money on baby paraphernalia?"

"Sure, I'm all for hitting the mall, it's better than solving crime," Penny laughed.

"Okay, you two get this dog and pony show moving. Keep me informed. I have to slip out before Weber catches me and makes me go back to my desk."

Deacon was looking a little green around the gills, as they say. I asked, "Shall we go start our mastermind plan?"

"May as well, I'll need the overtime income to pay for my enjoying sex," he grinned and we left the office.

*

Chapter 19

Deacon said we could take a car from the motor pool. I knew he wanted the Dodge Charger, his favorite vehicle. "What's wrong with my van?" I asked him.

"Nothing, if you don't mind traveling in a mobile house. Besides we get more respect in the Charger than in a motorhome," he replied.

As we got to the car, my cell phone buzzed, it was Angelo. "Angelo, what's up?"

"Mr. R, you doing anything really important right now?" he said sounding breathless.

"Are you alright, Angelo?"

"Oh, I'm fine. I just need to have you come over to my restaurant to give an opinion. If you can?"

I thought a second, looked to Deacon, then said, "I'll be over in a few, where is it?"

He gave me the directions and I hung up. "Deacon, I have to leave you for a bit, I'm needed elsewhere."

"No problem, I'm just going to talk to the D.A. for a wiretap warrant and see what our legal aspects are. Is it serious?"

"Not sure, it was Angelo asking for my opinion. He's opening a new restaurant and I hope he's not having any problems. I'll call you when I'm finished." I turned back towards my van, leaving Deacon to his toy.

I followed Angelo's directions and pulled into the huge parking lot next to the nice looking building.

Lipstick Murders

It had an Italian atmosphere to the outside décor, painted Italian flags and paintings of Italian scenes. It gave me a good feeling as I walked up to the door. It was a huge ornate door, nice dark wood and brass fittings. I was surprised that it wasn't heavy, it turned out to be thin.

I entered the dark room, not well lit yet, I presumed too early to waste electricity. I heard a voice in the dark of a side room and Angelo popped out to greet me.

"Mr. R, thanks for coming. I wanted to have you take a look and give me your honest opinion of the place," he said, with a big grin.

"Thank you Angelo, for asking. Give me a tour." He took me around the building, first in the dining areas, then the bar. It was a fine place, well decorated. Made me wonder why the last owners didn't make a go of it. We walked through the kitchen, modern equipment and well stocked. All shiny and new.

"It looks like you could be ready to open soon," I said.

"I'm hoping in two weeks, I still need staff. Plus, I got advertising starting this week in the Review-Journal and on late night TV, when people are up and wanting a snack or a drink."

"What about the liquor license? Are you going to be able to get that, with your past connection to the family?" I asked, knowing any underworld connections could queer a deal for the license. Sinatra had a problem like that.

126

"I'm getting around that, I have a silent partner, who's going to get the license for me."

I was a little concerned about this silent partner and asked.

"Don't worry Mr. R, he's a good guy. He's a lawyer who had minor connections with my late father's troubles. He's clean and a friend of the family, but no connections to show him dirty. He has some pull with the right licensing people and assures me we'll be ready by opening."

"Well, I'm glad for that then. I see a great place to start your venture as a restaurant owner. Have you figured out the menu yet?"

"I got a girl coming in; she's a graphic designer and is going to work up a nice menu for me. I got some good recipes from my mom and I've made out the selection of foods."

"Angelo, I will say, my money is being spent well. It looks good. I'm sure you're going to be busy in the kitchen, do you have a manager yet?"

"I contacted a local employment agency and they are sending a few people qualified in restaurant management. I'll have one selected by the end of the day."

"Good, just be cautious. Anything else you need me for?"

"Nope, I just wanted you to see the place and hear what you thought. Thanks."

"You know Penny and I support you all the way on this, and we expect special treatment when we come to eat," I laughed.

"Dinner's on me," he replied.

"Nope, I pay, you have to make money on this. No free rides. But you can buy me a few beers."

"It's a deal," he smiled.

"Okay, I have to go rescue Deacon on his case of the murdered models."

"Oh yeah, how's that going?"

"Rough, but we have leads to pursue and we have suspects. I'll fill you in more later," I said and started to head for the front door, stopped and turned, "You know we could put out the word that police are welcome here, they spend good money."

"Mr. R, come on, I'd be panicky around too many cops," he laughed.

"Got it, I'll talk later then," I said and left.

~~*~~

Buck was relaxing in Laynie's dressing room when the man entered. Buck stood quickly and blocked him. "Can I help you?" Buck asked menacingly.

Laynie yelled to Buck from the back of the room, "He's okay, Buck. He's my agent, Brian Anderson."

"An agent, eh? I'm still going to be watching you, Brian Anderson."

The man gave a guarded laugh and went to Laynie as she approached. They exchanged fake showbiz kisses and she invited him to sit.

"Laynie, are you still being harassed by the stalker?" he asked.

128

"Not since Buck has been watching my body."

Brian glanced over to Buck, he was sitting quietly by the door watching the man. Brian shifted in the chair and asked, "Are you happy with the arrangements here?"

"They aren't bad, the people who work here are friendly, the crew is helpful and the place is clean. Better than that casino in Kansas you had me in."

"That was not the best deal, but we needed the money. I have you in a sweet club in Los Angeles next."

"Sounds good, I've always like Los Angeles," she replied.

Buck suddenly felt a presence at the door and he stood quickly to face Earl Daws.

"Earl, what are you doing here?" Buck asked with a smile.

"Lacey filled me in on your case. I'm a big fan of Miss Keller's music. I thought I'd come by to see if I can help."

Laynie saw Earl standing at the door, and she saw that Buck knew the man. She came over and stood next to Buck.

"Buck, who is your handsome friend?" she beamed.

"Laynie, allow me to introduce you to one of our investigators at my firm, Earl Daws. He's a dangerous man, experienced in killing people, with a minimum of fuss."

Earl and Laynie both laughed and then Laynie invited Earl to come in. "Earl, this is my agent, Brian

Lipstick Murders

Anderson." The men shook hands. "Are you here to protect me Earl?" Laynie asked hopefully.

"I'm not in security, that's Buck's department. I'm in investigation. Since you have a stalker, Buck has to watch your body all day, but I can investigate who may be the suspect. If you have no objections?"

"I don't, as long as you check in frequently. I still have five days to perform here and I don't want to end up dead or tied up in some nut-case's basement. I feel safe with Buck and his men, I'd feel safer with you on the case."

"You got it, I have some free time. I'd be more than happy to investigate." He turned to Buck and said, "Shall we confer on the stalker, so I can start."

Buck grinned and said, "You got it."

~~*~~

I drove over to where Deacon said he would be. I saw the Charger parked and the space next to it was open so I pulled in. I stood in the parking lot of the county building, studying the structure. It was a typical government building, plain and stiff. I entered and was stopped at the entrance by security guards with wands that beep when they detect weapons. I opened my jacket to show my Glock and pulled my ID. They studied it, then they asked my business.

"I'm here to see LVMPD Sergeant D'Angelo, who is here to see the D.A. and I see him right there," I said pointing to Deacon standing with two men in the hallway. Deacon glanced over and called to the guards that I was with him. They passed me through.

130

It's really sad that we have to go through all this extra security to visit a lawyer. Then again, I would like to see a few lawyers murdered, so I guess they have to be careful who they let in, including me.

"Jim, this is District Attorney Mick Roberts. Mick, this is the famous Jim Richards."

"Ah yes, your reputation preceded you. I'm also a fan of your wife, Penny Wickens."

"Thanks, I'll tell her. What's the word?" I asked Deacon.

"We'll be getting a wiretap warrant on Harden's phone, based on Amanda's testimony. Next we inform Harden that he's losing his big star in this show. It should make Harden do something. We're hoping it will be a call to, or from, the mysterious killer."

"Well, it's all we can do for now," Roberts said. "Let me know what happens and I'll have the warrant delivered to your office."

"Send it to Lynn, she's running the show from her desk."

"She still suffering from her pregnancy?" he asked.

"Truthfully, I'm the one suffering," he grinned and we left.

*

Chapter 20

"You know, we could be going at this all wrong?" I said as we left the county building and went to our vehicles. "We are putting all our focus on Harden, but do we really know if he's behind this? What if we're wrong? We assume Amanda is the object of this to win the contest. The killer could be just someone who hates models and is still going to kill again."

"Oh, thanks for that," Deacon growled. "Although, that notion was bouncing through my head. I'm not liking it, but maybe we should focus on the other models. Since Amanda is hiding out, the others would now be the main target if you're right. I need to talk to Lynn, get her take on it. I'll meet you back at the precinct," he said and went to his car. I followed him to LVMPD and parked in the back, as he put the Charger back in the motor pool.

We found Lynn and Penny in Lynn's office going through some bags of baby stuff. I stayed outside the office looking through the windows. Deacon hesitated, but went in. Lynn held up a pair of booties, non-sexist in yellow. I could see Deacon turning green.

"That's nice, dear. Now can we get back to the case at hand?" he asked. He spent the next few minutes repeating our day and then sat, waiting for Lynn to speak.

"Very good, bunny bear, now the case is yours. I'm taking a few days off to relax with Penny. We're going swimming in her pool and shopping and talking babies. You are now the primary on the Lipstick Murders case."

I could almost hear Deacon groan quietly, but said, "I'll be able to take care of it for you. I'll need you to inform everyone about your decision, so they don't walk all over me."

Lynn yelled out loud, "Warren!" A few beats later Greg came to her door and said, "Yes?"

"Deacon is now primary on the Lipstick Murders case, so don't give him a hard time and tell everyone else out there my orders."

"Sure, Lieutenant, I'll let everyone know." He went off as Lynn looked to Deacon, "Is that good enough?"

Deacon had gone about two more shades of green and said, "I'll take care of it."

Lynn stood and gathered the bags of goodies and said to Penny, "Shall we go? I'll drive."

Penny stood and kissed my bald head and said, "See you back home. Don't go shooting yourself or messing with any models, or I'll shoot you," she smiled and left with Lynn.

"Okay genius, what do we do now?" Deacon asked me.

"Investigate! Of course. Shall we let Harden know he has lost his meal ticket?"

"I'm all for seeing him squirm." Deacon stood and went out to Greg Warren's desk to ask him a question. I came up behind.

"Greg, did you drop off Amanda Dawson at her friend's home."

Lipstick Murders

"Yep, I even took a tour of the place to make sure there were no bad guys around. It's a nice apartment, in the Koval Road area by Flamingo. It's tucked away and I gave them advice about avoiding trouble."

"You did inform her to lay low and not talk to any of her friends about where she is?"

"Yep, and I put Williams outside the apartment to watch them."

"Good, that will keep him out of trouble, too," Deacon laughed.

"That's why I did it."

"Okay, keep in touch with Williams to make sure they are all right, at least until I talk to Harden and see how badly he gets upset about her disappearance. Call Larry in electronics and have him get get a tap on Harden's phone ASAP. Here's the number," he said and handed him the warrant with the number. "I'll call you later to see how everything is going."

We said our good-byes and went out the back again. I volunteered my van, he hesitated looking towards the motorpool. I was sure he wanted to use the Charger again, but he yielded.

"Don't you ever take out the Crown Vic anymore?" Deacon asked as he buckled in.

"Actually, I was thinking of parking the van and using the Vic for my travels around the city. Gas is getting too expensive and this thing uses too much for the amount of mileage I drive it. Probably tomorrow I will put it to rest for a bit, save on wear and tear so we can use it for travel."

Deacon was looking towards the back of the van, "It's nice taking your home with you, but it is a bit big to be chasing down criminals. Now the Charger would be better to use."

"Why don't you sell that monster truck you have and buy your own Charger?" I asked.

"Actually, I thought about it, but Lynn figures with the baby coming, we need a family car, not a wild sports car."

"So a soccer-mom mini-van is in your future?" I laughed.

"Yep, that's the plan." Deacon sat quietly as I drove back to Harden's office.

Deacon pulled out the phone number for Amanda and dialed. She came on after a few rings, "Amanda, this is Detective D'Angelo, are you comfy in your friend's place?"

"As comfy as I'll ever be. I don't like being away from the runway and the clothes, but I realize that you have to catch the killer."

"Yes we do, now please don't answer your phone if Harden calls. I'm sure you have caller ID?"

"I do, and I don't really want to talk to him right now, anyway. You let me know when it's safe to get my life back to normal."

"I'll do that. We're on our way to his office now to let him know you are out of the contest, and see what he does. He'll probably try and contact you, don't let him. As I said, just wait until you hear from me."

"No problem, and thanks," she said and hung up.

"I think that girl is not as dumb as she looks. She seems to have it all together."

"Shall we put her up on the suspect list? She has much to gain, if she wins. She knows this whole charade is to throw off Harden and she wants to dump him anyway. Maybe she engineered this whole crime," I said.

"Again, you come up with the things that worry me."

"I'm sorry, but my mind keeps exploring the situation and we need to cover this case from all angles. You don't want Lynn to think you can't handle it? Do you?" I asked.

He paused thinking, "No, I may not be the best detective in the squad. I was always a cop back in Michigan and when I came out here, Lynn did most of the investigating. I just followed her around and gave muscle to solve the crime. Now I have to think, and it's not my favorite thing to do."

"Deacon, we've been on a whole lot of cases together, you've always come through in the pinch. Don't put yourself down, you are a great detective."

We pulled into Harden's parking lot and I asked, "How do you want to handle this?"

"I'm going to play it by ear. We'll see what happens," then he continued, "but pull my butt out, if I start messing up."

"You'll do fine. Lets' go." We exited the van and went to the building. The same receptionist was there from the last time we were here. She smiled at us and asked if we wanted to see Matthew.

"Please, we have some news he may not like."

She gave him a puzzled look and said quietly, "Are you arresting him?"

Deacon suppressed a laugh and said, "No, just some bad news about his chances of being a super-agent."

"Well, that works for me also," she smiled and called Harden on the phone. She waited for him to answer, then told him we were here. She paused again making faces, and then hung up. "He's not happy to see you here. He doesn't want to be disturbed."

"Is he alone?" Deacon asked.

"He is. I think he's just working on his computer, or watching porn."

"Thanks," Deacon said and went to the door. He opened it and we went in.

"I said I didn't want to be disturbed!" he shouted at us. Deacon went right up to his desk and glared at him. He shrunk in his chair a little and asked, "What do you want now?"

"We have some unfortunate news for you." Deacon pulled a chair over to the front of the desk and sat. I stood behind him looking tough. Or trying to look tough, I was never much good at it.

"What kind of unfortunate news?" he asked.

"Well, Amanda informed me today that she feared for her life and wanted protection. I told her we couldn't do much, but she should hire extra bodyguards. She decided to leave Las Vegas and drop out of the contest. She didn't want to be murdered. She wanted to be away from you and the contest without causing too much attention. I told her I would talk to you and explain the situation."

Harden went pale, looking shocked. He stood at his desk and was clutching his chest. He made a number of groans and chortles, that we couldn't understand. I presumed he was having an attack of something. His heart? He stumbled around the desk and went to the sofa in his office. He collapsed on it face down and was starting to shake.

Deacon was about to go to him, when he turned over, stood and screamed, "How could that bitch do this to me, after all I've done for her."

Then he collapsed to the floor, unconscious.

*

Chapter 21

The paramedics were making Harden as comfortable as they could on the gurney. They determined he had an anxiety attack, but wanted to take him to LV Medical for testing to be sure it didn't get worse. We stood watching the medics wheel him out, as his people stood around with smiles on their faces. Probably hoping he was going to die.

"Well, that sure took the wind out of his sails. You'd think he was faced with the greatest calamity ever to happen," Deacon said.

"It may be. If he did contract to murder the other models, he wasted a lot of time and probably money on it. Not to mention the contest loss. I'm sure he'll pull out of this, but what will he do then?"

"The medic I talked to said he'd probably be out tomorrow morning. I hope he comes back here to make any phone calls or we wasted a good wiretap warrant. So what do we do now?" Deacon wasn't sounding very happy and I knew nothing I could say would brighten his day right now.

"We wait. Isn't that what all good detectives do when a case is not leading much of anywhere," was all I could say. "Besides, it's getting late and this day was a busy one. We could go eat dinner or go home. Of course, Lynn is probably at my home so I think we should both go to your home."

That got a smile from the big man, "Call and see what the women have planned, then we'll go from there. I'm thinking we should go to a strip club and get drunk."

"I'm for that. I'll call Penny and see what's up." I pulled my cell phone and speed dialed her. She came on after a couple rings.

"Penny's home for unwed mothers," she said.

"I certainly hope not. Besides, Lynn is not unwed," I replied.

"She said she will be, if Deacon doesn't solve this case. And you can go live with him, too."

"Thank you, I love you too. Now what are your devious plans for this evening?"

"Lynn is ready to go home, so tell Deacon that is her plan. As for me, Angelo invited me to go to his restaurant to have a look. I told him I'd wait for you."

Lipstick Murders

"I've already seen it, it's nice, but we can go look together. I'll be home shortly." I made kissy noises on the phone and hung up. "You are going home, to your wife. Get some rest and keep track of Harden. You need to call Warren to see if the girls are behaving."

"I'll call on my way home. Take me back to the precinct so I can get my truck. I hope Lynn is rested from her swim and will sleep well tonight."

~~*~~

Buck was again in his seat by the stage for Laynie's evening show. Earl was walking around the room, scouting out people. Buck figured he was watching for any suspicious men sitting alone. The room was nearly full, lots of couples dressed for a nice evening of food and entertainment. Earl came around the side and sat next to Buck.

"Where are your two gorillas?" Earl asked.

"They're watching Laynie in the back, until she gets on stage. Then they will go out and stand at the back of the room."

"What are your plans for watching her in her hotel room? I'd gladly take that task."

"Oh, I'm sure you would, but it's me and Laynie. If you want to stand guard outside her door, fine with me."

"I presume you sleep on the couch?" Earl said with a big grin.

"Of course, I'm a professional, and don't get tangled up with my clients."

"But the alternative of hooking up with her would be nice."

"Don't think I haven't thought of it," Buck grinned right back.

The room light dimmed and the spotlight beamed at the stage. The band brought up Laynie's intro music as the curtain parted and Laynie came out to applause. She went into to her opening number and then continued through the whole set until the final bow. She smiled to Buck and Earl and went back through the curtain. Her show was about an hour and it went by fast. She had one more show to do so she needed to change.

Buck's men were already backstage and watching her carefully. Buck and Earl went through a door to the side of the stage and went to her dressing room. They saw the two men watching her door as Buck went to knock. There was no answer.

Buck tried the door but it was locked, something Laynie said she wouldn't do. Buck started banging and heard nothing. Earl brought his leg up and rammed his foot into the door as it gave way. The two men cautiously entered the room with their weapons drawn. Laynie was not there.

"Shit!" Buck cursed as he went to the back of the room, checking the bathroom. He looked to his right and saw another door behind a rack of clothes, he went to it and opened it. It was a short hallway, leading to another door with an exit sign on it. Earl came up behind him, along with the two guards, as they all went out the door. It was an alley and it was empty. Buck stood grumbling and looking around for any sign of what happened. He saw a door open and a man came out with a trash can heading to a dumpster. The men rushed over to him.

"Hey, have you been in this alley in the last ten minutes?" Buck asked.

"Yeah, I have to bring out the trash from the kitchen. Why?" the man answered.

"Did you see a car or truck parked over behind the stage door?"

"Yeah, it was a crappy looking Ford van, late eighties. It was painted really weird. It had rainbows and stars on it. I only looked for a moment, I had lots of trash to dump, so didn't waste time. It was just strange. I figured it was part of the show people."

"That was in the last ten minutes?"

"Yeah, it was about ten minutes ago. I came out five or so later, and it was gone."

"Thanks," Buck said and turned to Earl. "I need to call the cops and let them know to watch for the van," he said as he pulled his cell phone. "This bastard was quick. Grabbed her and out in less than five minutes."

He paused as someone came on the phone, he asked for help and explained. He finished and looked to Earl. "What do we do now?"

Earl looked around the alley and then saw a camera on a pole aimed at the back of the building. "Shall we go to the hotel security and see if they have a working camera there?"

Buck looked up to the camera and smiled, "It's something." They went quickly back into the building.

~~*~~

I picked up Penny and changed vehicles, taking the Crown Vic out of the garage.

"Are you slipping back into your childhood," she asked as she got into the car.

"No, just giving the van a rest, no sense in wearing it out before we go on a vacation," I replied.

"That and the cost of gas, I'm sure. It's nice to be more reclined while traveling," she said as she patted the comfortable seat.

"You could have gone in the back of the van and laid down on the bed while we traveled."

"Oh sure, then you'd come back and ravish me."

"Ravish? That's fancy for having sex, right?"

"I like ravish better, sounds so romantic. You're a writer now, or so you say, and you have to use fancy words to make your readers keep reading, right?"

"I guess ravish would peak their interest. But most of my readers would prefer sex. It's blunt and to the point."

"I'm sure your readers are forgiving, or they would be reading better books."

"And what's wrong with my books. They are selling quite well."

"When you make your first million, let me know." She sat back and watched the scenery, as we went to Angelo's restaurant.

Angelo showed Penny around, as I sat at a table by a nice big window, watching the traffic going by on Flamingo. A few cars would pull into the parking lot, read the sign Angelo put out front for his grand opening, and then drive off. He would have a good thing here, I thought. My cell phone buzzed and I answered, it was Deacon.

"What's up, Dad?"

"Not yet, please. I just got a call from Williams. He was watching Amanda and her friend, when someone approached the building, went up to their door and stood listening. Williams got out of the car and quietly approached him, but he turned, saw Williams and ran off. Williams swears the man had a gun in his hand, although it was semi-dark. There's something going on. Who would have known where Amanda was staying, Harden couldn't have. Is the killer still out for blood?"

"I'm at Angelo's restaurant right now with Penny. Are you going to investigate?"

"I'm thinking of it, Lynn is in a mood and I think I may want to be out of the apartment. But I think Warren can handle it with Williams, I really should be with Lynn tonight."

"You're a good man, Charlie Brown. Give her a little TLC and put her to bed. If you have any chocolates it may help too. Call me if you get anything more."

We finished and I hung up.

"Well, this makes for an interesting twist," I said to myself.

*

Chapter 22

"What's an interesting twist, Sweetie?" Penny startled me from behind.

I took a breath, "Oh, Deacon just called and said someone may have tried to get at one of the models, even though she's in hiding. Supposedly, no one knew where they were but Deacon, me, Warren and Williams."

"Yes, that does sounds like an interesting twist. But I'm sure you and Deacon will get to the bottom of it, won't you?"

"I hope so. We still need to catch the Lipstick Killer. Or shut down the contest, either way people won't be happy."

Angelo came up and said, "So Mr. R, you don't need me to work for you guys now?"

"Angelo, you are a self-employed man now, free of the bonds of employment for a boss," I laughed.

"One is never free of a boss, I'm my own boss now and I'm tougher on me than any boss would be."

"Very wise, Angelo. Just be easy on yourself, so you don't go quitting your new job," I said. "Are you on schedule to open when you want?"

"So far, so good. I have more people coming in tomorrow to interview. I have about half my crew hired and will start training, day after tomorrow."

"Good, now I have to take my lovely wife home and put her to work," I grinned, and stood.

"You're not my boss, so don't even get bossy. I am the boss of my own self," she grinned back.

Lipstick Murders

Angelo laughed and said, "I'm going to prep the kitchen and finish painting the men's room, so let yourselves out and see you later." He went off and I led Penny out of the building to the Crown Vic.

As I started to drive out, my cell phone buzzed. I stopped the car and answered, it was Buck. "Hey big guy, what's up?"

"Jim, Laynie was taken, from under our noses. Four body guards and she's gone. I'm in hotel security waiting to see the video of the van she was taken in. I just wanted to let you know the situation."

"I'm sure you'll be able to take care of it. Is Earl still with you?"

"Yep, he's not happy about this, as am I also. We're about to see the video of the van now, so I'll get back to you." He hung up and I sat looking at my cell phone.

"What's wrong, Sweetie?" Penny asked from her seat.

"There's so much going on, I need a vacation," I moaned.

"Is old age getting to you?" she laughed.

"Oh, hell no, I still feel like I'm thirty. Well maybe forty. I'm just feeling like it's getting harder to follow all this action. Model murders, missing singers, and who the hell is behind it all. I sometimes worry about things like memory loss or Alzheimer's."

"There are tests for Alzheimer's. Does it really bother you?" she said putting her hand on mine.

"I definitely don't want to forget you." I smiled, started up the car again and drove out.

We got back to our home and Willy was going nuts. Lacey must have dropped him off. She knew where we kept the spare key and how to reset the alarms.

"Poor baby, did we leave you alone?" Penny talked baby to him. He yipped and went to his food bowl. "Okay, you aren't scarred for life, I see." Penny went to get his kibble out and poured it in his bowl. She came into the bedroom where I was already undressed and under the covers.

"Aren't you even going to crack a beer and watch TV?" she asked.

"I just want to cuddle and get some sleep," I replied.

"Wow, you are getting old."

"Stop that, I am not, I just want to spend some quality time with you without beer or TV."

"Quality time? Does that include sex?" she gave me an evil smile.

"I'm laying here naked, you decide."

She reached to the wall switch and shut off the bedroom lights.

~~*~~

"We've been through about an hour of video, why aren't we seeing the van?" Buck asked.

"With thousands of cameras around this place, and they don't have the same set-up most of the big casinos have, it's a hit and miss," Earl replied.

"Finally found the alley," the security tech said. We moved in for a closer look.

147

Lipstick Murders

"There it is, the van with the stupid paintings on it," Buck said, then looked to Earl, "How can LVMPD not see that van on the roads?"

"Maybe he didn't have to go far, he was off the roads before you called. Can you get a close-up of the plates?" Earl asked the tech.

"As best as this equipment will allow," he replied and zoomed in on the plates.

Buck grinned as the plates came in focus. Earl wrote down the numbers and pulled his cell phone.

"Who you calling?" Buck asked.

"Harold Kettering," Earl replied.

"I remember him, your FBI buddy who helped us on the ship cruise to Tahiti." He looked at his watch and said, "It's after midnight in Washington, D.C., aren't you going to wake him?"

"Harold never sleeps, besides, if he is, I'll enjoy waking him," he paused, "Harold, this is Earl, did I wake you?" He put on the speaker phone.

"Earl, you always pop up at the worst times." Harold said over the phone.

"Having sex with an intern?" Earl laughed.

"Shut up Earl, what do you want?"

"Do you know who Laynie Keller is?"

"One of my favorite singers, why?"

"She's been kidnapped and I need a quick ID on the plate of the van that took her."

"You couldn't get the LVMPD to get that?"

"We just got it and they don't move fast like you do. Now can you help?"

"What's the number?"

148

Earl gave it to him and heard Harold making a few hits on a computer keyboard, Earl figured. "Were you surfing porn when I called?"

"Earl, shut up or you can wait for LVMPD. I'm doing this for Laynie, not you. Okay, here's the info and address. You ready?"

"I'm always ready, shoot."

"I'd love to, but my gun doesn't work over the phone."

"Quit wasting time, what's the info?"

Harold gave Earl the name and address of the van owner and Earl thanked him, then hung up. He looked to Buck and said, "Shall we go take down a kidnapper?"

~~*~~

About forty minutes after Penny turned off the light, we rested in each other's arms. Sex with Penny, despite her just turning sixty, was great. She pushed herself up on one elbow and looked to me in the light of the bathroom, coming into our room.

"I'm glad to see you haven't forgotten how to make love. Have you been exploring the internet?" she smiled and kissed my nose.

"Yes, a good number of porn sites, there's so much to learn. Amazing how many positions there are."

"You haven't read the Kama Sutra?" she asked.

"No, shall I go get the book?"

"I don't think you'd survive through the first chapter. We do alright without it. Now we need to get some sleep." She cuddled and then put her head on my shoulder and sighed. I sighed also, and slept well.

Earl was raring to go. He and Buck got into Earl's new Hummer and he roared out of the Silver Slipper parking lot. Buck had gotten the location of the home of Frank Mostafa from hotel security and the directions to the house. Buck navigated as Earl drove. Buck's two guards were in the back seat, chomping to get at this guy.

"Shouldn't we call the cops to help?" Buck asked.

"Maybe after we take this guy down and get Laynie back. The cops won't let us go into the house without a warrant. We have our own set of rules, and if this guy walks the courts, we'll have our own justice. The main point is getting Laynie back safely. If Mostafa gets hurt in the meantime, well, that's the breaks."

Buck sat back and smiled.

The house was secluded from the neighborhood, on its own, with the nearest neighbor about two blocks away. Earl pulled up to the driveway, but didn't pull in. He stopped the Hummer and they all exited the vehicle.

"Okay there's the van, we have the right place. Let's be careful here, we don't want Laynie hurt," Buck spoke quietly.

Earl gave instructions for the attack and they carefully went up to the house. It was dark except for lights in the basement windows. Earl went up to one window and peeked in. He whispered to Buck, "Can't see anything yet. Try the next window." They went down and looked in. They could see a man sitting on a chair at a desk, staring at a computer. They couldn't see what he was looking at, but he was definitely interested in something. There was a door to what maybe a cellar, it had a lock on it.

"Now, why would anyone want to lock a cellar door? Afraid of escaping pickle jars?" Earl asked Buck.

"I certainly hope Laynie is in there. She said the other day she hoped she didn't end up dead or in some pervert's basement. I feel I failed her," Buck lamented.

"Well, you'll save her and she'll be grateful, so let's take this bastard down." Earl said and stood.

They went around the back and Earl used his lock picks to open the door. They quietly entered and found the door to the basement. Earl went first. He could see the back of Mostafa and the computer screen. He saw what the man was looking at, it was Laynie's website. Earl pointed it out to Buck as he crept up behind the man. Buck went to the locked door and waited.

Earl coughed and the man about went out of his skin. He jumped up as Earl put a fist to his throat and the man went down. Buck fired his gun at the lock and pulled open the door. It was dark, but the light from the outer room they were in, showed Laynie huddled in a corner of the room. Buck went to her slowly, as she looked to him, her eyes went wide and she stood.

Buck went to her and put his arms around her, "You're safe now, I'm here."

*

Chapter 23

Earl had Mostafa bound to a chair as the officers from LVMPD came rushing down the stairs. Buck had taken Laynie up from the basement and the EMS techs were checking her. They couldn't find anything wrong, just nerves. Laynie waved them off and called Buck to come to her for support.

"This wasn't the way I wanted to have you catch my stalker," she said with a smile, sitting on the EMS truck step.

"But we did catch him, now you are free to perform without worry. But for safety sake, I'll hang around for a few more days to be sure, at no charge," Buck smiled back.

"Hell, I'd still pay you to just hang around for the fun of it. Can you be sure he's the stalker?"

"Earl went through his computer while we waited for the cops and he found the emails that were sent to you. So it's a safe bet he's the one. Oh, and your last show was canceled, with apologies. So you can just go back to your hotel and get some needed rest tonight."

"Are you still going to be around?"

"If you want."

"I do, please take me to the hotel," she said and stood slowly.

Buck asked Earl to take them back as Earl finished with the cops. He drove them back and dropped them at the front entrance of the hotel, and then he went home to Paula. Everyone was in for the night.

~~*~~

I was making my morning toast as Willy was munching on his kibble. Penny was humming as she whipped up her oatmeal.

"Damn, I miss Angelo and his great breakfasts," she said.

"Didn't you learn anything from watching him?"

"I was more interested in eating the food, than cooking it. We may need to start our day with breakfast at Angelo's now."

"I didn't see a breakfast menu, but he likes to cook breakfast, so it will probably be coming soon. I just hope he does well," I said.

"As long as he keeps prices down and the quality of his food up, he'll do fine," Penny said, between a mouthful of mush.

My cell phone buzzed, the ID said it was Deacon. "Good morning. Is Harden out of the hospital yet?"

"Yep, about an hour ago. I have Warren on his tail and the wiretap is working. All we can do is wait now."

153

Lipstick Murders

"Any more problems with Amanda?"

"Nope, it was a quiet night, Williams switched off, during the night, with a couple other detectives and all reported nothing happened."

"Do you want me to join you at the precinct?"

"No, take some time to relax and I'll call if something breaks."

"Good, I'll go into my office to see what's happening there. Talk to you later."

I hung up and ate my toast, while Penny rushed around getting ready to go interview stars and celebrities on her talk show. It was doing well in the ratings; people liked her and the way she ran the show.

"I'll probably stop by your office after I'm finished at the studio. Are you going to be in?" she asked.

"I don't know. It depends on what breaks in the case. Either Harden will make a mistake, or Amanda will be in danger. It could go either way. Oh, and I have to see how Buck made out with Laynie and her kidnapping. Exciting stuff," I said trying to sound upbeat.

"I'm glad you're in a better mood, I was worried about you yesterday."

"I'm fine, just a little run down. I need to get more exercise."

She stood looking at me and laughed, "You need to cut down on burgers and beer. Your weight is what's running you down."

I swallowed my toast and said, "I'll start tomorrow."

"Yeah, right," she said and kissed me good-bye. She went out the door to the garage and drove her car out. I looked to Willy, he was looking back up to me.

"Are you ready to go fight crime?" He wagged his tail, as I went to get my things to go out.

I drove the Crown Vic to the office and parked in front. I came into the outer lobby and greeted Tracey. "How are you today?"

"I'm good Mr. Richards. Lacey gave me a bunch of papers to organize to keep me busy," she replied sounding very chipper.

"Great, have fun with that," I said and went into the inner lobby where I found Lacey at her desk, with papers all around her. She looked up and said, "Buck needs to keep up with his guard reports. I really shouldn't be doing this. Can you get him to hire a secretary of his own?"

"I'll talk to him about it. He may like having a personal secretary. Any messages?"

"Nope, you are being ignored this morning."

"Good, I'm going into my office and closing the door. I prefer not to be disturbed, unless we get attacked by models again. The female kind I mean."

I went through the glass door to the private offices. Buck's door was closed, as was Earl's. Will Trapper's door was open and I went to it. He was sitting at his desk reading a paper.

"I thought you were going out of town with Samantha?" I asked, as he looked over to me.

"I did, it was just an overnighter to see her brother, I mean, new sister. She's doing well after the sex change, getting more feminine every day. I

155

wouldn't be able to tell, if I didn't know the whole story."

"I'm glad she fixed her situation. How are you and Sam getting along?" I asked.

"We're on a steady course, no commitments, just boyfriend and girlfriend for now. You know friends with benefits sort of thing."

"I could never see how people could maintain that kind of a relationship. Sex gets in the way every time."

"Well, we both aren't interested in a definite commitment, so we get along just fine. How's your case coming?"

"Slow, I'm waiting for Deacon to call - if he gets something from a wiretap that we have on our main suspect. This is such a waiting game, not like the cops and private investigators on TV."

"It would be nice if we could solve our cases in an hour," Will laughed.

"Yep, talk to you later," I said and went to my office. I put Willy on the floor, he shot right back out to go visit with Lacey. We installed a small doggie door for him to get from the front to the back of the building. That way we weren't constantly having to open doors for him.

I sat back in my chair looking at Penny's picture in the bikini. I had fond memories of that ship cruise. My cell phone buzzed, it was Deacon.

"Hey boss, what's up?" I asked.

"Well, a hit was tried on Amanda about an hour ago," was all he said. I about fell back in my chair.

156

"Talk to me," I said, catching my breath and my balance.

"Williams was sitting outside the apartment relaxing, when the girls came out to go do laundry in the apartment laundry room. As they were walking along the walkway on the second floor, a shot rang out hitting the wall of the building, just missing Amanda. Williams called for back-up and jumped out of his car, running to the building. He saw a car with a man inside holding a rifle, and he pulled his revolver and aimed at it, but the car drove off. This is not good, Jim."

"Okay, where are you?"

"I'm at the apartment building, Warren is going over security video of the parking lot. Are you coming by?"

"It's five minutes away, I'll be there." I hung up and stood, going out of my office and went to the front. "Lacey, an attempt at murder was just committed, I have to go, watch Willy." I stormed out the front door, before she could respond, to where I left my car and drove out.

This was really messing up our theory, why would Harden want to kill Amanda? Is the mysterious caller on Harden's phone wanting to murder her. He said he had money on her, why blow that now? Could it be another contestant wanting to get her chances up better? How did they know where Amanda was? So much, so little. I pulled into the parking lot for the apartments and saw the black-and-whites all over. I saw Deacon up on the second floor with Amanda, they were looking out to the area around the building.

I got out of the car and was stopped by an officer at the crime scene tape. Deacon saw me and yelled to the officer to let me pass. I went up the stairs on the side and came around the front of the building to where they were.

"Jim, this is all puzzling. Why would this happen?" Deacon was looking distressed.

"Well, maybe we have to change our direction. It could be another model in the contest who's doing this," I replied.

"Hell, Jim, that doesn't make sense, if she kills off all the other women, we'd know who it is. Last woman standing."

"True, and it doesn't make sense that there are even murders to take out the heavy hitters for the win. This could be just some psycho who doesn't like models."

"Again, you are making this harder."

"But they are all good theories, we have to look into everything," I said.

I turned to Amanda and asked, "What's your thoughts on this? Who would want to kill the models?"

She paused, then said, "I have no idea. I just don't want to be another body on a slab. I'm really out of here. Illinois, here I come."

*

Chapter 24

I stood looking over to the area where Williams said the car sat. "I'm puzzled," I said to Deacon, as he stood next to me waiting for me to speak. "The killer took out the model in the Fashion Show Mall from much further than this is. But we believe he was shot at next to a dumpster. Is this shooter not as good, or…" I looked to the spot on the wall where the bullet hit. It was high and way off from where the women walked. "Is this just a bad shooter or a diversion?"

"Diversion?" Deacon asked.

"Well, from the place where the shot came from, it isn't that far, even I could hit a target like Amanda from there with a decent rifle. Could this be not a hit, but a warning?"

"Warning? Talk to me Jim."

"We have no idea how anyone found out where she was staying, but if they did know, maybe the shot was to tell her to get back in the contest or die."

"I would think she would be warned about that," Deacon said. "The killer would give her the details for the attempted hit."

"Yes, let her know they could find her and kill her if she didn't continue with the contest. Harden could have engineered that."

"We're waiting on the wiretap to see if there's any plot to do that. Plus he didn't have the time to set this up. He was just released from the hospital this morning."

Lipstick Murders

"We need to talk to Amanda," I said and walked around the big guy to the apartment where the women were resting.

Both girls were sitting on a couch; Amanda's friend was comforting her. I went to them and asked, "Amanda, I need to ask you a few questions."

She looked up and I could tell she had been crying. I looked to the friend and said, "And you are?"

"I'm Beth Erwin, I've known Amanda for years. This is all so disturbing."

"Yes, it is. We need to get some facts together to hopefully catch the killer. Amanda when you came here, did you tell anyone?"

"No, I told no one. The only person who knew I was here was Beth, other than you cops."

I looked to Beth, "Did you tell anyone that Amanda was staying here?"

She looked away, a sign of deceit for most people when asked a question.

"I told no one."

"Are you sure? We can check your phone records to see who you talked to."

Her eyes grew a bit, then she closed them. "No, I told no one she was here." She paused, then said, "Okay, I may have told a friend that she was here. Just one friend and he would tell no one."

Deacon stepped forward and asked, "I need the name of this friend, and where we can find him."

Beth hesitated, "I don't want him to get in trouble."

160

"Well, he may already be, so you'd be better off telling me or go into the station and answer questions there. Now, you want to cooperate?" Deacon said, trying to sound tough.

She looked to Amanda, and started to tear up. "I'm sorry Amanda, I didn't want to do it."

"Do what?" Amanda asked.

"Turn you in to them, but they suggested that I could be hurt."

"Who are they?" I asked.

"The men who make big bets, the mob," she said and broke down. Amanda comforted her.

I looked to Deacon, "I can't see the mob getting in on this, betting on what's basically a beauty pageant."

"They bet on anything, I've learned that being in Vice. I'll call the Organized Crime Unit and see what they know," he said and turned to Beth, "I need a name, now."

She wiped the tears running down her face with her hand and said, "I'm sorry, his name is Sebastian Welsh, he's with the Bochino Family out of Reno. I met him a few weeks ago, and he found out I knew the models in the show. When Amanda disappeared he called and asked me if I knew where she was. I didn't want to tell him but he threatened me. I was scared, you have to understand."

"How could he know that she was missing, we just set up the sting yesterday?" Deacon asked.

"You'll have to ask him. He didn't say."

"Where do we find him?"

Lipstick Murders

"All I know is he likes to hang out at the Sicilian Social Club over on Durango. I heard him talking about the place on the phone," She sniffled.

"Sicilian Social Club? If that doesn't sound like a mobbed up place, I don't know what would. Do they actually do that anymore?" I asked.

"Jim, these older mob families like to keep hold of the past. And they use names that are meant to bring fear into the hearts of people."

"I'll have to talk to Angelo about this, see what he knows," I paused, then, "It makes sense, that Harden got a phone call about this. They were bold enough to scare him into submission. Any word on his wiretap?"

"None yet, at least I haven't heard anything. I'll call in a while," Deacon answered. He turned to Greg Warren, standing at the door, and said, "Greg, take some men and go over to the Sicilian Social Club on Durango and pick up Sebastian Welsh. Bring him in."

Greg acknowledged and left. "We have to move the women, for their protection." Deacon said to me.

"I'm thinking that maybe Amanda should get back into the contest," I said.

"Why?"

"Well, she wouldn't be in any danger. They'll protect their interest. And we may be able to draw out the people involved."

"Hey," Amanda yelled from the couch, "I just said, I was not hanging around here, don't think you can get me to compete in the contest now. Someone just tried to kill me!"

I went to the couch and sat next to her. "Amanda, if they wanted you dead, you would be dead. I think this was just a way of telling you to get back in the contest. Look, someone has a lot of money riding on you to win the thing. They wouldn't hurt you, if anything you are going to be protected now. If the mob is behind this, no one will touch you."

She sat staring at me. She finally blinked, "Are you certain of that? Are you going to put yourself in front of me next time someone takes a shot at me?"

"We'll put your bodyguards back on you. They make a pretty good size wall around you."

She actually cracked a smile at that and then said, "What about Matthew?"

"We'll keep him in the dark until tomorrow. We still need to get any evidence on him, if he is involved, or just a patsy for the mob."

"All right, but I need to move somewhere else, just to be sure," she said.

I looked to Beth and smiled, "Yes, and somewhere alone."

Beth looked like she was going to cry, "I'm sorry, I didn't mean to tell Welsh, he threatened me. I need to be taken somewhere safe too, until this is over."

Amanda moved over to her and put her arm around her. "It's okay, you can go with me." She turned to me and asked, "Can we take her, too?"

"Only if she doesn't use a phone or have contact with anyone." Deacon spoke now. "The LVMPD has a safe house that we can take you both to. Just until tomorrow night and we have proof that you both are in no danger. The contest is the day after tomorrow, we'll put you back in the contest tomorrow with an announcement. You'll still stay away safe until the day of the contest and with your bodyguards."

"It works for me. If I get killed, I'm coming for you," she smiled and pointed her finger at Deacon.

He cleared his throat and said, "I'll go arrange to move you two, get packed with just what you'll need." He turned and went out.

I stood and said, "Don't worry, we'll be careful now that we know a little more of what's happening."

I followed Deacon out and saw him talking to Williams down by the cars. I went down the stairs and over to them. Deacon turned to me just as Williams went off with a couple of patrol officers, to get the women from the apartment.

"They're going to take them to the safe house. Do you really think this will work? What do we have so far?"

"Nothing, and I have no idea if this will work. But I have faith in you and we have only two more days to finish this. Let's see what the wiretap is producing."

"I can do that. I'm tired of being around models," he said, then yelled up to Williams standing by the apartment door, "We're going back to the precinct, take care of them."

Williams called down that he would and we left. I followed Deacon to the station and parked.

"I'll call Warren and see if he found Welsh. Maybe we can get something out of him." He stopped in the parking lot before going in, "I hope Lynn went home to rest."

"You really are on edge with her, aren't you?"

"It's like living with Jekyll and Hyde. One minute, she's sweet and loving, then she's a raving lunatic. I've never jumped so much in the last month or so.

We went in and came around a corner to the squad room, when we heard a loud voice, "Deacon, get in here!" He jumped.

He caught his breath and said, "See, I told you."

*

Chapter 25

"You had Warren raid a mob social club?" Lynn said firmly.

"No, I had him go pick up a suspect in the Lipstick killer case. Why? Did it turn into a raid?"

"Well, the family and their lawyers aren't happy. What has this Sebastian Welsh done?"

"He was the only person to know the location of Amanda Dawson and I feel he had something to do with the attempted shooting of her. Amanda's friend Beth fingered him for the possible set up."

Lynn sat back and smiled, "Good, bunny bear, now go question him. It's your case now, I don't want to stress myself."

Lipstick Murders

Deacon looked to me and shrugged, "Care to join me?" We went out of Lynn's office and Deacon said quietly, "See? Jekyll and Hyde."

We went to the interrogation room where there was a man dressed in a nice, black sharkskin suit, sitting with another well-dressed older man, probably his lawyer.

"Sebastian Welsh?" Deacon asked the sharkskin suit.

"Yeah, why am I here?" he replied with a snotty attitude.

"Mr. Welsh, we just want to question you in regards to a possible attempted homicide. We haven't arrested you, you're just a possible suspect."

"Suspect? I didn't try and kill anyone. I've been with friends all day," he shot back.

"Yes, but you knew where the victim lived. You were the only person besides myself and a few cops who knew where she was hiding out. You know a Beth Erwin?"

"I have an acquaintance with a Beth Erwin, yes."

"You talked to her yesterday and badgered her into telling you where Amanda Dawson was staying."

"Amanda Dawson? The model? Now why would I want to know where she is? She's supposed to be competing for the big ass model competition. What does that have to do with me?"

"Ms. Erwin said you talked to her on the phone and demanded that she tell you where Amanda was."

"Well, how do you know she's not lying?"

"I have no reason to doubt her, considering your record of being involved with the Bochino Family."

The expensive suited lawyer spoke now, "Detective, all you have is the word of a woman who may be lying. Besides, there is no connection with my client to the Bochino Family."

"Oh, we pulled him out of a social club owned by the Bochino's and you are on their payroll. I think that speaks volumes as to his connections to the family."

"If my client is not under arrest or a suspect, we will be going."

"Your client can't have a nice talk with us to help an innocent woman from being murdered? How's that look for the Bochino's public relations?"

Welsh spoke, "I'm more than happy to help. I don't murder women or contribute to their murders. What is it you want?"

"You knew where Amanda Dawson was staying, from the phone call. Who did you tell after that?"

"Okay, Beth was all thrilled about having Amanda staying with her and told me about it. I didn't badger her into telling me. I just called to see how she was doing and she volunteered the info. Honestly."

"Okay, but did you tell anyone else?"

"I may have mentioned it to a few of my buddies at the club. We all sit and talk about things. We were talking about the model contest, and I may have bragged about knowing where one of the contestants were staying. Not illegal, or improper, just trying to out-do my buddies. I had no idea she was in hiding, Beth didn't mention that."

Lipstick Murders

"It was in the papers this morning that Amanda had dropped out of the contest, because of fear for her life. You, or your buddies, don't read the papers?"

"Of course, I think that's why I was pleased that I knew where she was. But I didn't rat her out to anyone."

"We have reason to believe that there may be big money riding on her participation in the contest. Maybe big mob money?"

"Now why would the family, if I knew them, not saying I do, have anything to do with betting on a glamor contest. Shit, the family has enough money to keep them going for years without placing their own bets."

Deacon looked to me, then back to Welsh. "Can you give me an idea of who might place a big bet and may have murdered three models to put Ms. Dawson up to win."

"I can't answer that," he said.

"Can't or won't?" Deacon asked.

The lawyer spoke again, "Detective, my client is cooperating, let's not be accusatory."

"It's okay Oscar, I'll answer the detective's question, I don't know. So I can't answer," he said with a grin, "There are more bad guys out there than me, not saying I'm a bad guy. You could check every bookie joint in town, they may have better answers for you."

"Okay, Mr. Welsh, you can go. But I may need to talk with you again." Deacon stood and went to the door, opened it and waved his hand to let the men know they could leave.

After Welsh and his attorney left, I said, "I could talk to Trapper's paramour Samantha about the betting scene."

"Paramour?"

"Yeah, look that up in your Funk and Wagnalls," I replied with a sly grin.

"Fine, don't tell me. Let's go talk to Larry and see if Harden has said anything interesting."

Deacon made sure not to pass Lynn's door as we made our way to the crime labs. We found Larry and two other detectives listening in on Harden's phone calls.

"Deacon, I was just going to call you. Unless Harden is using his cell phone, we're getting not much about the killings from his office phone. He did get one call asking where Amanda was, he said he didn't know. It was someone from the network producing the TV coverage of the competition. They weren't happy about losing another contestant. Harden said he'd call them when he found out something. So far we have nothing."

"Thanks for making my day, Larry," Deacon said sarcastically, then turned to me, "Shall we go visit Trapper's paramour?"

As we were walking out, he asked if paramour was a fancy word for bookie. I said no.

In the parking lot by Deacon's unmarked car, I called Trapper to see where Samantha might be.

"She's with me right now. We're having a bite to eat, care to join us?" he said.

"Sure, what burger place are you at?" I asked.

He laughed and said, "I can afford better than burgers, we're at the Ocean Breeze."

"Oh, I see, fish fillets instead of burger patties," I laughed.

"Hey, this is a nice place. No fast food here. Now what do you want?"

"We, meaning Deacon and I, need some info on big betting for the model competition. May we join you?"

"Only if you buy your own fish sandwiches," he replied.

I hung up, and looked to Deacon, "Are you interested in fish?"

We arrived at the restaurant and found Will Trapper and Samantha enjoying some kind of fish on a metal plate. "Looks good," I said, until I saw that the fish still had the head attached. "Doesn't it bother you to eat a fish as it watches you back?"

Trapper laughed and said to sit or leave. We sat.

"Hey, Sam. Is this lug treating you okay?" I asked her.

"He knows better, or I cut him off from the one thing he enjoys the most," she replied.

"Television?" I said.

"You and Penny enjoy TV, we enjoy pleasures of the body. Now do you have a reason for interrupting this perfect evening?" Will grinned, as he picked at the middle of the fish's body on his plate.

I grimaced and said to Sam, "We have a small problem. We need to know if there have been any big bets placed on Amanda Dawson to win the model competition."

"You don't ask for much do you? Besides, what makes you think I would know, I have nothing to do with placing illegal book on events," she said with a sly smile and a glance to Deacon.

Deacon cleared his throat, "I'm going to look the other way on the situation. We're in a bind here. Now if, I say if, you would know, have there been any big bets placed?"

"Well, if, and I say if, I would know about this fact, I'd talk to Bernie Lessel, he takes the really big bets. I'm sure there had to be really big money on this since there was murder committed. These people aren't messing around. If Amanda wins, there would be a big million dollar payout. But I don't know about these things."

"Bernie? Isn't he mobbed up with the Bochinos?" Deacon asked.

"That's what I hear. I don't get involved with the mob. They don't play nice. Besides, I have Will to protect my interests."

"Boy, has he steered you wrong," I laughed.

"I may hire him away from you to run my security. He's already run off a few people who wanted to muscle in on my turf." She put her hand on his and patted it.

"Really, I haven't heard about this?" I said.

"I don't go around bragging about my adventures like some people, who write books about them."

"I included you in my books, I made you look good."

"Yeah, you did. I still haven't gotten the royalty checks for my mentions," he smiled.

"The check is in the mail," I replied.

"Yeah, yeah. How's the case going?"

Deacon spoke, "Not great, we have too many suspects, and not enough evidence. But we need to talk to Bernie now. Maybe it will help."

*

Chapter 26

"Bernie is a decent guy, unless you don't pay your debts. He is tied into the Bochino family, so he has a bit of clout, be careful," Sam warned us.

"Where do we find him?" Deacon asked.

"There's a used book store over on Pecos, just north of Bonanza. He sells more than old books."

"I'm sure we'll find it. Anything we should know about him?" Deacon asked Sam.

"He loves hard candy, lemon is his favorite. You could sweeten him up and maybe he'll give you what you need. You can mention my name, we are on a friendly basis."

"Thanks, I think we'll pass up on the fish," Deacon smiled, as he eyed the fish head on Trapper's plate.

"You just don't know what's good for you," Trapper laughed.

"If I don't get something on this, my head will be on Lynn's plate," he said and looked to me, "Ready to go?"

"Yep, I've lost my appetite too," I replied.

We said our good-byes and left the restaurant. I stopped in the parking lot and said, "I'm thinking maybe we need to take a side trip. To get some info from my favorite mob man."

Deacon smiled, "Angelo. That may help, and I'd like to see his new place."

Deacon drove over to Angelo's restaurant and pulled into the parking lot. There was a sign company truck hoisting a nice big sign saying "Mama Mia's Italian Restaurant" up to the front of the building. It was a nice sign, well decorated and bright. Angelo was standing by watching the men work and then came over to us as we exited the car.

"Mr. R, so good to see you again. Hey Mr. D, how's crime fighting?" Angelo held out his hand to Deacon, they shook.

"Crime is crime. Hard to solve and hard to avoid," Deacon replied.

"I need to pick your brain, my friend," I said.

"Shoot, I'm a fountain of information," Angelo laughed.

"What do you know about the Bochino family's connections here in Vegas?"

Angelo stood watching his sign being put in place. He was quiet for a moment, then said, "We need to go inside and talk." He walked to the building, we followed.

"Please sit." He pointed to a table and went to the bar area and got a bottle of some kind of wine, and three glasses. "I know you drink beer, Mr. R, but this calls for a good glass of vino."

173

Lipstick Murders

He poured the drinks and sat. "Now, you want to know about the Bochino family? They are a modern type of family, not the old school, but into more technology than breaking legs." He grinned when he said that. "I know a couple people in the family, they are old relatives, more my age than the youngsters who are running things now. It's sad, but all the real mob families are growing up and being taken over by the kids. Not like it was in the old days."

"Do you know a Bernie Lessel?" I asked.

"Bernie? Sure, he's okay, he's old, but he's one of the new crew. His method of booking is all computer now. He doesn't break legs, but he can hurt you worse. He uses blackmail and extortion by computer now. Amazing what can be done now days to ruin a man. Just a simple chirp on the computer, and you are outed."

"I think you mean tweet," I corrected.

"Yeah, that too. Now what do you want with Bernie?"

"We need to find out if anyone has placed a huge bet on Amanda Dawson in the model competition," Deacon said.

"I don't know if Bernie would divulge that information. But since we know each other, maybe he would tell me. Give me a minute and I'll go with you." He stood and yelled for someone named Henry.

A couple seconds later, a young man came out of the back and went to Angelo. Angelo turned to us and said, "This is my new shift manager, Henry Hull. Henry, these are two good friends of mine, you see them again, you treat them with respect. This is Jim

Richards, PI and the big guy is Deacon D'Angelo, a homicide detective."

"Good to meet you, gentlemen," he said.

"I'm going out for a bit, watch the sign people to make sure they do a good job."

"Will do, boss," he smiled and went out.

Angelo turned to us and said, "Shall we go into the hornet's nest?"

The three of us went to Deacon's car and drove out, Angelo giving directions.

We arrived at a simple red brick building nestled between two larger buildings, housing a gym and a boutique. Deacon parked between the buildings and we went in. There were two rather large men at a counter, by the front door of the used book store.

One of the two saw Angelo and grinned. "Hey Angelo, what's up?"

"Hey Max, need to see Bernie, if he's in?"

"For you, always." He picked up a phone and made a call. He hung up and made small talk with Angelo. A few minutes later a door opened towards the back and a man came out. He motioned to follow him.

On the way through the store, Angelo said to Deacon, quietly, "I'm not going to introduce you as a cop, it will make everyone nervous. I'm going to introduce Jim as a PI, and you're his associate. Let Jim ask the questions."

Deacon said, "That's fine with me."

We went through the door into a larger room, with about a dozen men at computer terminals, reminding me of Samantha's bookie joint. The man led us to an office and we all went in.

"Angelo!" said an older man seated behind the desk. He stood and came around to us. Angleo and the man hugged and then he asked, "What brings you to my business? You wanna place a bet?"

"Bernie, you know I don't bet. I have just a small favor to ask."

The man was eyeing Deacon, then looked to me. "I smell cops. Angelo did you bring police to me?"

Angelo kept cool and laughed. "Bernie, this is Jim Richards, private investigator and his associate Deacon D'Angelo. They have a case and need some info."

"Richards? I've heard of you. You smashed the betting scam during the big World Series of Poker tournament, that would have cost Samantha Hathaway a cool million." He looked to Deacon, "D'Angelo? You Italian?"

"Yes sir. My full name is Francis Albert D'Angelo. Named after the great Sinatra."

"Ah, yes. Good to meet you both. Now what can I do for you? Come sit." He pointed to chairs nearby; we pulled them over to his desk and sat.

"Mr. Lessel, we're working the case of the murders of the models in the model competition. We believe that the person who is behind the murders has placed a rather large bet on Amanda Dawson to win. They unbalanced the outcome by killing the leaders in favor of Amanda. We just wondered if you could help us by letting us know if a big bet was placed with your… uh, firm."

Lessel smiled, "I understand what you're going for. It would be in my best interest to stop this bet, as the outcome was, as you say, unbalanced. But unfortunately there has been no bets placed here for this woman. I do follow the papers and know who she is. As far as I know, no book has been placed on her anywhere else. I can't help you, sorry."

I sat back, depressed that this lead went down the toilet. "We've had some talk about the Bochino family being interested in the contest. Do you have any thoughts about it?"

"The Bochinos are good to me, I don't step on their toes, they keep off mine. We have some ties, but nothing I would talk about. I know of no interest that the family would have in this competition. They are busy with too many other irons in the fire. Whoever told you this was not well informed."

"That helps a great deal, Mr. Lessel. We can now rule out the garbage. Oh, and Samantha Hathaway said to say hi."

He grinned, "You know Sam?"

"She's dating one of my associates, yes, we know each other."

"Ah yes, I heard she was dating a former cop. Interesting."

"Will Trapper was a former cop in Michigan and here in Vegas years ago. He's now licensed private with my firm."

"Trapper? I knew a Vegas cop years ago named Mike Trapper, any relation?"

"Yes, Will's father. He's passed on now."

Lipstick Murders

"So sad. Have Sam and Will come by one day, I have some stories to tell him about his father."

"I'm sure he'd love that, I'll tell him. Thank you so much for your time, we'll let you get back to your business."

Angelo spoke, "Bernie, I'm opening up the restaurant I told you about, in a week. I'll have a table reserved for you, so let me know when you can make it."

"I'll do that my friend, thank you." We all stood and followed him to the front of the store. He and Angelo embraced again, "Say hello to your mother for me," he told Angelo.

"I will Bernie, thanks," Angelo replied with a smile.

We went out to Deacon's car and drove off.

"Angelo, if I didn't know better, I'd think you were starting your own little family out here," I laughed.

"No thank you, I still keep in touch with the families that are friendly to mine, but that's as far as I want to be. Just friendly. But it never hurts to have the right connections."

"Yes Angelo, I enjoy those connections, too. It makes my investigating much easier," I replied.

*

Chapter 27

We pulled into Angelo's parking lot and I got out as Angelo exited from the back door of the car. I stood waiting, then went to him.

"Angelo, I have depended on you so many times to help me solve crimes, you are, and always will be an important part of my life. Thank you my friend, and the best to you in your new venture. I'll be here to help you with anything you need." I went to him and gave him a big bear hug. He embraced me and then moved back.

"Mr. R, you are a great friend. You don't care if I have criminal connections; you always treat me fair and are a true friend. I would lay my life down for you." He looked a bit misty and went off towards his building.

I slid back into the car as Deacon started to pull out of the lot. "You two had a moment there didn't you?" he smiled.

"Other than Buck, Trapper, Earl and you, there aren't many people I would trust with my life. Angelo is towards the top of my list. He treats his friends as humans, and would do anything for them. I remember how I first met him, his mother sent him to guard Penny and me during the Bridezilla murders. He didn't know us, but stood by faithfully and kept us from harm. I never forgot that."

"He was a handful as I remember. If not for him and his connections, we wouldn't have caught the killer," Deacon said wistfully.

Lipstick Murders

"So, what do we do now?" I asked, to change the subject before I choked up. I looked back to the restaurant and saw Angelo standing outside looking at his new sign. He looked happy.

~~*~~

Buck had spent most of the day with Laynie, they were now back in the dressing room as she was getting ready for her show. Earl had stopped earlier to see if all was well. Buck said they were satisfied that the stalker was in custody, but he was hanging around for a while longer. Earl left and Buck asked Laynie if she was feeling comfortable now.

"Yes Buck, I am. Thank you. You have done your job well and above the call of duty."

"Well, I need to get back to my life. I'm sure my lady is wondering what happened to me. I'll leave one man with you, just in case. But I feel it's over now. I've enjoyed watching you, you are a true professional and a great singer."

"Thank you again Buck. I'll miss you."

Buck went to her, sitting at her dressing table, bent over and kissed her forehead. "Thank you for being you," he said and went out of the room.

~~*~~

"Hell, we got nothing," Deacon moaned, "The mob isn't involved in it, Harden hasn't tipped his hand and I don't think he will. All our leads are crap now. CSI hasn't come up with any evidence as to who may

180

have pulled the murders. Lynn is going to have a cow now."

"Look, who has the most to gain in this? Think about it?"

"Well, we know Amanda will come out smelling like a rich rose. But could she have engineered this whole thing?"

I was watching the road and thinking, "Why not? If she had friends in the right places to pull the murders, why not?"

Deacon was quiet for a while, I didn't want to interrupt his thought process. "I can see it now. She has been steering us towards Harden, maybe to get us off her track."

"It's a thought. She's the only person who will benefit from all this," I said.

"She wanted to break away from Harden, who would she have gone to? Who would be her new manager or agent?"

"Maybe the Lansome agency?" I said. "Could they be helping her to win? I never liked that woman, Kate Lansome. She seemed deceitful to me. Maybe we need to talk to her again. She doesn't know Amanda is hiding out and it was reported that she was out of the running. Maybe we should see what reaction she has?"

"I like your way of thinking. It's getting late now, but she should still be in her office. Shall we go see? I'm all for that, Sherlock," he said with a grin.

"Very good Watson, elementary."

Lipstick Murders

We arrived at the Lansome agency again after Deacon turned the car around. He parked and we went in.

The receptionist recognized us and said, "I know. You want to see Mrs. Lansome."

"Mrs.? I didn't know she was married? Who's her husband?" I asked.

"Walter Lansome. He's rich and patronizes her hobby. She owns the agency but he foots the bill. I'll tell her you're here." She lifted the phone and placed a call.

I looked to Deacon and smiled. "We have another suspect. Money talks to rich people," I said quietly.

The girl said to go in, we did. Lansome was at her desk sitting up smartly and watching us enter. "Do you have good news for me?" she asked.

"Depends on the news. Did you know that Amanda pulled out of the competition?" Deacon asked.

The look on her face would have made me wonder if she was going to have an anxiety attack also.

"You didn't know?" I asked.

"No, I hadn't heard. When did this come about?"

"Late yesterday. Didn't Matthew Harden call you about it?" Deacon asked.

"No, he hadn't. He knew about this?"

"Yes, but he was struck with an anxiety attack and ended up in a hospital until this morning. He's fine now, back to work. I would have thought he would have called you." I said.

"No, this is the first I've heard. I'm surprised that Amanda hadn't called me about this."

"Why would she. You weren't her agent."

"Well, we were friends at least. She often called me to talk about her career."

"Speaking of her career, did you know that she wanted to leave Harden and go with another agent?" I asked.

She paused, searching for words. "Well, she had mentioned that."

"Wouldn't you want her to join your team?" Deacon asked.

"Well, of course. She was a treasure in the modeling world. A gem that needed proper guidance, something Matthew couldn't give her. He didn't understand the female psyche and how to mold it to its full potential. To become a real model in this miserable world of fashion. I knew how to do this, I told Amanda that she could come to us anytime she felt Matthew wasn't doing his job."

"Had she expressed any desire to join you?"

"She was thinking about it. Nothing definite. I wasn't going to push her to it, that was her decision."

"Well, she would have been worth millions to you if she had," I said.

"Mr. Richards, it's not all money in this business. I have scruples and wouldn't take advantage of her in any way. Is there a reason you are here?"

"We just wanted to know if you knew she was out of the running," Deacon said.

Lansome went silent again, "Do you know where Amanda is?"

"We do. Is that important?" Deacon asked.

"I'm just concerned for her safety."

"Well, she is in our protective custody. We wanted to be sure that no harm came to her before she went back to Illinois."

Lansome went a little pale and asked, "Is she really leaving Vegas?"

"That's the plan. Is this a problem?"

"If that's what she wants. I'd just like a chance to talk to her before she does something rash, like leaving the competition. She knows she would be a winner."

"But at what cost, her life?" I asked.

"She wouldn't have been harmed!" Lansome was in a panic now.

"And how would you know this?" Deacon asked.

"Uh… I don't know, but why would anyone want to hurt her. She's a pro, not like those other women. They weren't professional."

"I thought one of them, Tiffy, was one of your girls. Are you saying she wasn't a real model?"

"No, that's not what I'm saying. Tiffy was the best, she was going places. She wanted the best for herself, and I could give her that." She went silent.

Deacon sat watching her, then said, "Okay, we will be going, but we will be in touch. Thank you." He stood and I was surprised that he was cutting the conversation short. I stood and followed him out.

"What are you up to?" I asked him when we were out of the office.

"She said something that caught my interest, I want to follow up on it. Let's go track down some models."

We went to the Fashion Show Mall again and in to the trailer where the women were changing and getting ready to walk the catwalk. Mr. David was prancing around getting the women ready. Deacon went to him.

"Well Detective, are you a sight. Couldn't get away from me," he smiled at Deacon.

"I need to know who here is a model with the Lansome agency?" he shot out.

"Well, nearly half are, just point and it's a good chance they are one."

"I need one who likes to gossip, got one in particular?"

"Sweety, they all love to gossip. But if you want the queen of the bitches, talk to Marge Hokinan. She's over there." He pointed towards a redhead standing getting dressed in a flaming red gown.

Deacon went straight towards her and stood in front of her, flashing his badge. "Marge, you need to talk to me, now."

*

Chapter 28

Deacon seemed incensed and stood his ground with her, even though she protested his intrusion.

"I just need to talk to you, and then you can go back to your little show. Now, talk to me or go into the precinct and answer questions there."

She paused and then yielded, "Okay what do you want?"

Deacon pulled her over to the tables in the center of the room and told her to sit, he sat next to her. "I need you to tell me some truths, what was Tiffy like to work with?"

"Tiffy? She was a bitch. No one liked her and she wasn't a team player."

"Okay, now talk to me honestly, had Tiffy ever said she wanted to leave Lansome Agency?"

The girl sat quietly and then said, "She told me one day that she had a call from the William Morris Agency to go work for them. Yes, she was planning on leaving Lansome. But after the competition. She wanted to win, then take her glory to New York. If she hadn't been murdered she would have been out of here."

Deacon stood up and then turned to me, "Lansome may have known that Tiffy was leaving her agency. If Amanda wanted to join, Tiffy was a liability. Amanda would have won and it would be a feather in Lansome's cap to have her join. Tiffy was leaving, so who cared if she died. I think Lansome engineered this whole thing."

"I'm proud of you Watson, you've solved the case," I said.

"No, it's not solved yet. We need a confession. From someone." He turned back to Marge and said, "You can go back to work. Thank you for your time."

The woman stood and walked away. Deacon sat back in the chair vacated by the model. He looked tired.

"It's late, and there's not much we can do now, is there?" I asked.

He looked up to me, "I want this to end. I liked it better when Lynn did all the thinking. My life is changing, and it scares me. I'm becoming a father and I don't have a clue what to do."

"There's no manual for raising children, there's probably more instructions on crime fighting than being a father. I just went with the flow every day after my son was born."

"Either way, it's going to change. Like having to buy a soccer-mom van. I want a Charger, but we'll have to do the family route. Oh well."

"I think you need one of those energy drinks. Or solve this case and celebrate. Either way we have one day before the competition to catch a killer," I said, trying to cheer him up. I know Deacon is big and tough, but he has a gooey inside that needs hardening sometimes.

"Yep, we need to get our act together and work the case. What do you suggest now?" he asked.

"Oh sure, push it on me. What would you do if you were alone?"

"I'd go hide," he said with a big grin. "Okay, let's go do some checking on Lansome, and maybe her husband. We need to go back to the precinct."

"It's now just after five and I'm wearing down myself. Call Warren and let him do some fact checking."

"That's sounds like a good idea." He pulled his cell phone and called Greg and gave him the information. He hung up and looked to me, "Okay, I'm going home. I'm done."

Deacon drove me to my car and I went home. Penny had settled into the living room with some movie on. "Chick flick?" I asked, as I plopped down next to her.

"Of course, I need this to keep me going. You haven't been very attentive lately."

I just watched her face, waiting for the smile to crack. It did. I jumped her and we wrestled for a bit, "Hey, you're too old for this," she yelled.

"If I break a bone, you can drive me to the hospital," I replied, sitting up. Willy was bouncing around our feet, so I picked him up and put him on my lap.

"So, have you caught the killer yet?" she asked.

"Deacon's working on it. Although, I think he's losing his nerve. Between Lynn's mood swings and his insecurities about fatherhood, he'll be a wreck before the month's end. This case has too few options and too many suspects."

"I'm sure you'll figure it out. Now I'm tired and going to bed early. This movie is boring, so why don't you spice up my night?" She gave me her evil smile and went off to the bedroom.

I looked to Willy who made a face like he knew what I was going to say. He jumped off my lap, on to the couch and laid down to rest. He snorted as I got up and went to the bedroom.

~~*~~

The next morning, Deacon called and said that Amanda called him and asked if she could get back into the contest.

"I figured it was her neck, and Lansome would make sure she was protected. She's worth more to Lansome alive."

"What's the word on Harden?"

"Nothing. They are still monitoring his calls and Larry said he'd call me if anything develops. Want to meet at Lynn's office. She's not coming in today, pregnancy sickness, or whatever, is getting to her."

"I'll see you there," I said and hung up. Penny had already left and took Willy with her to work. Her make-up girls loved to watch the dog while Penny entertained her audience.

I finished dressing and gathered my items to take. I pulled the Crown Vic out of the garage and watched the van as I drove out the drive. It was a good looking van, we'd be taking more trips later when time allowed. I arrived at the LVMPD station and parked, going in to where I found Deacon standing by Greg Warren's desk. He was looking at some paper.

Lipstick Murders

"Hey Jim, got some goods on Lansome's husband. It seems he was accused of killing a model six years ago in a bad affair, but the case had no evidence and he had an alibi. So it was never closed." Deacon said, still examining the sheet of paper.

"So, he wouldn't have any qualms about killing again?"

"Maybe not. According to his financial's, he's getting very low on funds. The modeling agency hasn't been very lucrative lately. I talked to a few more models this morning, and they all said Tiffy was definitely moving on. Everyone knew, so I'm sure Lansome knew too."

"Where's Amanda?"

"She's being watched by Williams and a couple security guards from Buck. She's at the MGM Grand auditorium, where the competition is being held."

"Has Harden been informed that she's back?" I asked.

"I don't know. She would have had to call him if she was back officially."

Deacon's cell phone buzzed and he answered. He listened, then hung up. "Larry has something from Harden and needs us."

We went to the lab and found the tech still listening on the wiretap. "Hey Deacon, got something interesting for you, hold on." He fiddled with the keyboard on the computer and the speakers came on with Harden's voice.

"Hello?" Harden said.

"Matthew, have you heard, Amanda's back in the contest." The voice sounded like Kate Lansome.

"Kate, when did you hear this and why didn't I know?"

"Matthew, you should know something. Amanda is leaving you and joining my team. I just wanted to give you a heads up, before you get too excited about her being back," she said.

"What the fuck are you saying? Amanda would never leave me! Are you trying to start something with me? I don't appreciate it."

"No, Matthew I'm not starting anything with you. I'm finishing you off. Without Amanda you are nothing, you're firm will go broke and you'll be out. I'll be glad to see you go down in flames."

"You bitch, I'll fight you in court, I have a contract with her!" he screamed.

"It won't do you much good while you are in jail," she said coolly.

"What are you talking about?"

"I have it on good authority that you set up the murders of Tiffy and the others. I'm ready to give my info to the police."

"What the fuck are you talking about! I had nothing to do with their deaths, I figured it was you who set it up. Just like your husband killed Melissa back six years ago, to get rid of her for wanting to jump your ship. You are a crazy bitch and I'll see you in court! You got nothing on me!"

We could hear him slam the phone and the call went dead. "Interesting," Deacon spoke.

"I wonder what Kate has on him that would implicate him in the murders?" I said.

Lipstick Murders

"She may have just said that to shake him up. We still need Mossa Lefler to pull out of his coma and finger the person who set this up."

"In light of that never happening, we need to talk to Harden again. We may need to let him in on the wiretap."

"No, we can say we were tapping Lansome's phone, that way we can still listen in on him."

"Very true, see, you are sounding like a real detective now," I said with a grin.

"I'll take that as a compliment, let's go." He thanked Larry and we left the lab.

We drove back to Harden's building and found him sitting at his desk. The building was empty, no people around.

Deacon cleared his throat, bringing Harden out of his trance. He jumped and looked to us.

"Now what do you want?" he said meekly.

"Where is everyone?" Deacon asked.

"I fired them all, I can't pay them if I don't have any money. My agency is crumbling and it's Lansome's fault. But I'll get back at her. It's good that you're here."

*

Chapter 29

"I pinned my hopes on Amanda winning. It would have brought in a good cash flow. Now I find that she's deserting me. Going to Lansome."

"Matthew, did you plot the murders of the models?"

He looked at Deacon with red eyes, and smiled. "No, it had to be Kate Lansome, and her murderous husband. They saw the writing on the wall with Tiffy, she wasn't happy with them. She had better offers and was leaving Lansome. They don't like that. They don't care if they steal models from other agents, but God forbid anyone would leave Lansome." He reached to a glass on his desk, next to a whiskey bottle, took a big swig and poured another glass full. "I lost three models to Lansome, I didn't care, they weren't the best. But I had hopes for Amanda. It was fortunate that she is up for the win now. Even at the other model's expense. I'm sorry for them."

"What are you going to do now?" I asked.

"I'm going to talk to Amanda and see if I can get her to stay. She owes it to me, I found her and groomed her to be what she is. She owes it to me."

I actually felt sorry for the man. He looked so miserable sitting there. Deacon's cell phone buzzed and he answered. He listened, then hung up, turned to me and said, "We're needed at the MGM Grand." He looked at Matthew and said, "Please don't do anything foolish now. We have to leave, so just wait until we catch us a killer. You may still be able to save your agency."

Harden looked to Deacon and gave a brave smile. "Please catch Lansome in this. It's my only hope."

We left his office; it was so deathly quiet in the building as we moved to the front entrance. "What was the call? I asked.

"Williams, he said there was a problem with Amanda getting back into the competition. She needs an agent to qualify, Harden was her sponsor and they are not going to let her in without him. Lansome is saying she has taken Amanda as a client but that's not the way the rules work. Now Amanda is having a fit and Lansome is threatening everyone."

I stopped and said, "Maybe we need to bring Harden. Just to see if something will break."

Deacon stopped just short of the door, and turned. "Yeah, that would be a good idea. I knew there was a reason I keep you around."

We went back to his office and found him still sitting. Deacon informed him about the problem, Harden just laughed. "Matthew, you need to come with us. We may be able to clear this all up, and it could be to your benefit."

Harden slowly stood and went to get his jacket from a coat rack, he looked over to us and said, "I hope you're right." He went out to his car and followed us.

We arrived at the MGM Grand and went to the auditorium. We found Williams standing between Lansome and someone who probably was from the show. They were in a heated debate. Deacon went to them as Harden and I followed.

Amanda saw Harden, she looked a bit shocked, then frowned. Kate Lansome turned and saw Harden also. She came rushing to him and said, "You weasel, you need to get Amanda back in the contest," she demanded.

Harden just smiled and said, "The shoe is on the other foot now, eh, bitch."

Amanda came over and pulled Harden aside. "Matthew I need to get back in, you signed the contracts for me and they won't let me back without your signature. Please, Matthew I need this."

He stood for a minute, thinking, then said, "You were going to leave me? Why? What did I do to you but put you up on the pedestal for all to admire. I gave away most of my money to buy things to help you get where you are. I'm now almost broke and had to fire everyone who worked for me. They did it for you. How could you do this to them and me?"

"Matthew, I'm sorry, but I had to think about my career. You just gave me a push, but I needed someone with clout to get me to the top."

"You think Lansome can do that for you? They'd throw you under a bus if you started to fade. What if you don't win this thing, you think they'd stick with you?"

"Matthew, I'll try and help you financially, if you just sign the contracts for me. Please."

He looked to her and smiled, "I'll do it, but you will find out who your real friends are."

Lipstick Murders

He went to the table for the show's officials. He stopped and looked to Lansome. "You stay away from this, if you stick your nose into it, I'll pull the plug. Now be-gone witch!"

Kate Lansome moved away from the table and went to Amanda. Harden turned and yelled, "And stay away from her, now!"

Lansome looked lost, but moved aside to a tall man in a very expensive suit. I figured him to be Walter Lansome, by the way she was clinging to him. He didn't look happy.

Harden did what he had to do to get Amanda back into the competition. He didn't look happy, saying to Amanda, "You owe me." Then he turned and walked out of the room.

Both of the Lansomes went to Amanda and were talking to her. I followed Harden out and caught him sitting on a bench in the lobby.

"Matthew, what happened to all the other models you had?"

"They were all for show, I had only one client, that was Amanda. I hope she fails on her win," he said, trying not to choke on his words.

"Well, it's in the judges hands now. What are you going to do?"

"I'm going to sit in the audience and watch, hoping she trips on the catwalk."

I had to smile at that image, "I'm sure things will work out."

"You are an idiot if you believe that. The Lansomes are dangerous people, if they can't get what they want, they take it. Or destroy it. Watch them carefully. I have to go salvage my life. I'll be back later." He stood and walked out of the lobby to the street.

Deacon came out and sat next to me. "We still need to find out who set up the kills."

"I was thinking about that, but we need to talk to Amanda again. Can you pull her away from all the vampires?"

Deacon laughed and said he would. He stood and went back into the auditorium. A few minutes later he came back out with Amanda in tow. She didn't look happy. He instructed her to sit with us and looked to me.

"Amanda, you are back in the contest because Matthew agreed to sign, even though he knew you were abandoning him. I think he deserves a little thanks. You can help us catch who murdered the models and ease your conscience. We have a plan and unfortunately it means you have to help us again. I'm sure you want revenge for whoever killed Tiffy, don't you?"

She nodded and said nothing. I explained what I had figured we would do to draw out the killers. She sat nodding and finally agreed. Deacon sat smiling at my plan and then took her back to the Lansomes.

He came back out and said, "I like it, but do you think it will work?"

"I can only hope. Shall we go rest for the big show. I think Penny would love to come. Maybe you can convince Lynn to join us, too."

"I'll see how she feels. Now, first we need to get this set up with Warren and Williams."

197

Lipstick Murders

We both stood and went to find the detectives.

An hour later I was in my office, as Penny came into the room. "So you told Lacey to have me see you as soon as I arrived?"

"Yep, how would you like to go watch a big model competition?"

"Only if I get to judge," she said with a sly smile.

"Okay, what are you up to?" I said, knowing the look on her face meant she had something going on.

"Gordy got a call today asking if I'd be interested in being a judge to fill for someone who took ill. I said I would love to. Gordy called them back and arranged it."

I laughed and said, "So, you judged the Elvis competition last year and now you get to judge the babes. That's going full circle. Good, I don't have to worry about you then. Deacon and I have a sting going on and I may need to move around."

"Still trying to catch a killer?"

"We hope to wrap it up tonight, if all goes well. Can you vote in favor of Amanda Dawson?"

"Jim! That would be cheating. I'll vote fair and square. If she's good, I'll vote for her. Of course, there are nine other judges, so my vote may not swing a whole lot."

"Just do your best, you always do."

We went home to get dressed in evening wear and arrived at the auditorium around seven. Penny went off to go to the judge's table. I wandered around until my cell phone buzzed, it was Deacon. "Where are you?" I asked.

"Right behind you," he said, and I turned to see him standing with Lynn. She had on a gown that accented her pregnancy, she looked good. I went to them as Lynn asked where Penny was.

"She got railroaded into judging this shindig. I reserved seats for all of us behind the judge's table so we can be close. This should be interesting, and hopefully a close to it all."

We went into the auditorium.

*

Chapter 30

Deacon went backstage to check with Warren and Williams. They were ready to put our plot to work. Deacon saw Amanda behind the stage getting ready. She saw him and gave him a big smile and a wave. He came back out to us sitting in the front row behind the judge's table. Penny was right in front of us, she was twisting around to try and talk to us. Lynn finally stood and went to her, they chatted for a bit.

All around the auditorium were the camera crews that were going to transmit the show to the world, live. I always loved live television; it had a sense of danger. Would someone collapse with a heart attack, or get shot, live in millions of homes. I saw Matthew coming in and went to him.

"Matthew, come with me, I have a seat reserved for you right up front," I said.

Lipstick Murders

"Great, now I can be close to the back stabbing bitch."

"That's the spirit, Matt. You may enjoy this evening, we will have a show later, just stick with me." I took him to the seats and he sat on the end, next to Deacon. The big man introduced Matthew to Lynn, they shook hands cordially and then the lights were going down slowly.

From the center of the curtain a man came out and said he was the stage manager for the show. He explained a number of things that the audience would have to do to make the show work. Since it was live he asked everyone to remain seated during the show. He finished explaining the rules and said to be ready for the start of the show.

He went back through the curtain as the orchestra was starting to tune up. A big lit LED sign, high up, flashed saying two minutes till air time. Then it said one minute. The orchestra started the opening number as the sign said, 'On the Air'.

The curtain opened and there stood the ten models that would be competing tonight. The host, some good looking guy from one of the network talk shows came out and did the opening spiel, introduced the contestants and then moved forward to introduce the judges. There was a huge monitor above the stage, where we could see what was being telecast to the world. Penny's smiling face came on as she was introduced. I think she got the biggest applause of the judges, but I was prejudiced.

The show was underway now, first with each model introducing themselves to the audience.

Amanda held up very well. I could hear Matthew grumbling quietly from his seat. I hoped he didn't do anything stupid. I whispered to Deacon to keep an eye on him just in case. Lynn said she'd tackle him if he even moved. I had to laugh, because I knew she would do it.

For the next hour the show went smoothly, and the models did their best to make quick costume changes. Like they would for a fashion show. After another half hour the show was winding down. The host asked the judges to tally their votes and they would announce the winner.

The show went to commercial and Deacon and I excused ourselves to go get set up for our sting. I bent over to Matthew and said, "Just stay in your seat, we will catch the killer, but you need to remain here. Understand?"

He nodded and I went with Deacon to the backstage again. It was a little crazy, with all the people involved with the show and the crew working the stage. The Lansomes were standing off the side with Amanda. The girl turned to see us on the other side of the stage, she smiled.

"I hope this works," Deacon said.

"No more than I," I replied.

The show came back from commercial and the host had the results of the contest. The spotlight illuminated him and he spoke.

"Ladies and Gentlemen, this is the moment we all have been waiting for, the announcement of the winner of the first Greatest American Model competition. The winner takes home a cool million dollars and will serve as co-host for the Fashion World show on the Lifetime channel. I'm sure all the ladies are anxious to know who has become our winner, so I will announce them in order of last to first by score."

He opened the envelope and studied the list. "In the last four places are the following." He read the names of the losers as they went off the stage. "Sorry Ladies, but you all had high scores. Now I'll announce the next three models and then we will announce the winner." He read the next three models, leaving Amanda and some blond left. I could see Amanda looking scared even though she had a huge smile.

I saw the Lansomes on the other side holding on to each other. They looked hopeful. I knew that their firm was also low on funds, dangerously low, according to Warren's investigation. This win would put them back into the bucks. So I figured they were both wetting their pants a little.

The spotlight tightened in on the last two models. The host came over and gave them congratulations and then looked to the list again. He paused then said, "One lady will be the runner up and she will fill in if the winner can't fulfill the show hosting position. Now, the runner up is… " he paused for effect, I hated that. "Amber Franson, our winner is Amanda Dawson!!"

The crowd went crazy as all the models came back out on the stage to congratulate Amanda.

They put a crown on her head and gave her flowers. I could see Amanda crying. I actually felt happy for her, even though I didn't approve of her dumping Harden.

Deacon said, "Gee, we didn't see that coming, did we?"

"Let's go get into position," I said and we went around to the other side waiting for the show to end and everyone came off stage. It was amazing how the other models were ice cold now as they came through the curtain. Amanda came through last as the Lansomes rushed to her. They took her aside and were jumping for joy. We could see Amanda say something to them and they gave her a strange look.

"Here it comes, let's go." We went to them, but stayed back far enough to watch.

Amanda led them to a door off the side leading to a hallway with a number of doors. The hallway was empty.

We came to the door but stayed outside. We each put in the small earpieces that would let us hear the short range bug we had on Amanda. This bug was small but only good for about twenty feet to be heard. We listened.

Kate Lansome was so overjoyed, she sounded sickening. Amanda calmed her by saying she had something to tell them. They went silent as Amanda spoke.

"Kate, Walt, I want to thank you for having faith in me, but I have some news. Since Tiffy was murdered and she couldn't fulfill the offer the William Norris Agency gave her, they contacted me and gave me the same offer. So, I'm sorry, but I will be going with them."

Lipstick Murders

"What!!" Kate screamed. "No, you can't do this!"

"Well, they are a bigger agency than you guys, so I think it would be better for my career. I waited to see how the competition came out before I made a decision. I'm sorry."

Walter spoke now, "This is not acceptable, you can't do this to us after all we did for you."

I was hoping they'd admit to hiring the killers.

"Just what did you do for me Walt? Maybe I have the killers of the models to thank for my win. I had no chance with the other models out front."

We could hear silence then Walt spoke, I hoped for the right words. "I'll see that the Norris agency knows what kind of person you are. I'll pull in all my connections to ruin you."

Not what I was hoping to hear. Deacon's cell phone buzzed and he answered. He listened and was making faces. He hung up and looked to me, "Damn, we almost blew it. Follow me."

He went through the door with his weapon drawn, I didn't know what to do but I was ready to draw my weapon, in case. Everyone in the hallway looked surprised as Deacon came to Amanda and said, "Amanda Dawson, you are under arrest for conspiracy to commit murder and hiring hitmen to murder three women. Place your hands behind you."

A door off the side opened and out came Warren and Williams. Deacon told them to cuff her.

"Deacon what's going on?" I asked. Before he could answer he turned to the Lansomes and said to get lost, they would be told later what was going on.

The two of them left the hallway as Deacon turned to me.

"Well, I got my wish, Mossa Lefler came out of his coma long enough to tell the detective watching him that it was Amanda who hired him and his partner to murder Tiffy and the others. He's not happy that Amanda shot him by the dumpster. She thought he was dead, and never asked about him. She didn't know he was still alive." He turned to Amanda and said, "You commit crimes you have to cover all bases." He looked to Warren and said to take her in.

He turned to me and said, "You had a great idea, but she wasn't going to get any information from the Lansomes and she knew it. So she played along. This case is solved."

*

Chapter 31

The committee of the model competition was informed as to the outcome and they told Amber Franson that she would be the winner. The girl was delirious with joy. I saw Penny coming towards us and she gave me a strange look.

"So what's going on?" she asked.

"We caught the person who hired the killers and tried to kill one of the killers herself. It was Amanda," I said with a smile.

"So your plan worked?"

Lipstick Murders

"Well, actually no," I paused, "The killer who Amanda tried to murder, came out of his coma and fingered her. Just as we were trying to get a confession from the wrong people. Talk about close calls."

"So you didn't actually solve the case. It was handed to you by the killer."

"Don't rain on our parade. I want Deacon to take credit for the arrest and taking her in. Maybe Lynn will stop badgering him."

"No such luck, Lynn loves badgering him. Now can we go home, I'm all modeled out, too much beauty in one setting."

"I have one more thing to do." I kissed her and told her to go find Lynn and hang with her. I went off to find Matthew still sitting in his seat all alone. I sat next to him.

"Matthew, I didn't mean you had to stay here. I have some news to tell you. It's not good."

"Amanda hired the killers," he said quietly.

"Uh, how did you know?"

"I just felt it. I made up the calls from the killers, just to see what she would do. It didn't really faze her, so I figured maybe she was involved. I was hoping I was wrong but when she decided to jump ship, I didn't care. I hope she rots in prison."

"Well, she didn't commit the murders but she did shoot the man she hired, Lefler, and tried to kill him. So she may do a lot of time for attempted murder. If she's good she may be out before she gets too old. What are you going to do now?"

"I'm going to make peace with Kate Lansome and see if we can regroup. One agency may be better than two. Thanks for helping me today, I appreciate it."

I stood and said, "No problem, I hope you make it. Take care." I walked away and saw Penny and Lynn standing by the exit. The place was pretty much empty, other than reporters talking to Deacon and Amber. He looked like he was enjoying the attention of the press.

I went to the girls and stood as they were still talking about babies. Not a subject I wanted to discuss.

The evening finished up as we all sat in the front yard of our home, looking over the Vegas valley and the strip shining distantly in the night.

"Did you ever think it could have been Amanda?" I asked Deacon.

"Actually, I had her on my radar for a while, but Harden looked too good for being the criminal. How can such a sweet looking girl be so bad?'

"She wanted it all, and Matthew couldn't give it to her. She knew she couldn't win with Tiffy and the others, so she got desperate. I'm surprised she didn't follow up on Lefler, to be sure he was dead. What ever happened to his buddy Weasel?"

"Don't know, I have an APB out for him, he may turn up or maybe he's a victim of Amanda also. He had to have murdered the last girl, he probably was the photographer. Lynn thinks he was also the one who took the fake potshot at Amanda, she probably set it up to distract us. Lefler was the crack shot so he

207

took out the runway model. I'm tired of models now, I hope we never have to investigate them again."

"Yeah, but you have to admit, they were good to look at." I looked over to Lynn and Penny opening the trunk of Lynn's car. They had gone shopping sometime in the last day or two and left the packages in the trunk.

I saw a car coming up our road and it looked familiar, it was Buck's T-Bird. He drove in and he and Maria got out. They came to us, as Deacon greeted his sister, "No work tonight, baby girl?"

"Nope, my night off, Buck and I are catching up. He's spent too much time around that singer."

"Yeah, how did that go?' I asked.

"Earl and I found her, got her back safely. Did you catch your criminal?"

"Let's just say she fell into our laps?" I laughed.

Deacon grinned and said, "Yes, we got our woman. I'll tell you more about it later."

"Right now we just need to chill and enjoy the evening," I said as I raised my beer can.

THE END

~~*~~

Preview of the next book, "Pasta Murders"

Chapter 1

Angelo.

That name struck fear in the hearts of men who didn't pay their gambling debts on time to the Traviano mob family in New York. The mention of his name and the threat of a visit from him would make strong men cringe in fear. Angelo never actually touched anyone. He had men to do that. It was his job to see that people paid up or walked funny.

Angelo was brought up by his mother, Francis, the matriarch of the family. Ever since she was a young woman, she had been married to mob capos, two of whom died at the hands of rival gangs. Her newest husband, don Gino Traviano, ruled the illegal gambling operations in his territory and took on his stepson to enforce the rules he set down as to delinquent payments.

Angelo was actually a kind person, but he had an image to uphold. He wouldn't let anyone get out of paying.

Today, Angelo held a meat cleaver high over his head. He brought it down with such force that the blade cut cleanly through the flesh and bone. He grinned as he separated the meat and made a few more whacks.

Angelo was preparing steaks to be eaten in his new restaurant that he recently opened in Las Vegas. He had turned his back on being a leg-breaker for the family and, with his mother's and stepfather's blessing, moved from New York to Las Vegas. He first started working for Richards Investigation and Security as a celebrity bodyguard, then Jim Richards made him an offer he couldn't refuse. Jim fronted the money so Angelo could open his new restaurant, one he had wanted for a long time.

Angelo was preparing a special dish for a distinguished visitor to his newly opened establishment. A food critic from the Las Vegas Review-Journal newspaper was coming in to check out the place. Most the time this food critic wouldn't announce that he was coming, but Angelo had an inside with all the right people through his past connections to the mob. He got word the reviewer was coming, so he worked hard to make sure his visit was the best.

Little did Angelo know that the critic's meal in his restaurant would be his last.

~~*~~

It was a Saturday morning and I stood outside the Victoria's Secret store in the Boulevard Mall waiting for Penny to come out. She went in to buy a new bra she saw advertised on TV last night. She just had to have it. The ad promised that the bra would make her breasts pop out even more. But she didn't need much help in that department. She was well built.

Even though she was sixty, she still had a nice firm body, and her breasts still stayed north of her belly button. But she had to have this bra, so I endured going shopping with her, a job I never cared for.

I went to the benches they provided for weary husbands to relax while the wives spent their money. I didn't worry about money. I made enough from my book sales and from my investigations of husbands going wild. The detective work was doing well and, with Will Trapper and Earl Daws, it was actually fun. Buck had his security team of around 180 men. He was happy.

Life was good in the Vegas valley. Tourists were starting to flock in as the economy got better. I didn't have any more murders to investigate since the fashion show models were killed. I actually had a small respite since that case. Penny and I did a lot of exploring around the area, going camping a couple times on Mt. Charleston. Of course the motorhome van I owned was like living in a motel, so the word camping was not really descriptive of what we did.

"You're not supposed to be resting," came a voice to my right. It was Penny with bags in hand. She sat next to me and started to open the top bag. I had a feeling she was going to pull out the bra to show me. I didn't need that in public.

I reached over, put my hand on the bag and said, "You can show me later, even model it for me."

211

Lipstick Murders

"If you're lucky," she replied closing the bag. "Have you been sitting here all the time I was in the store?"

"No, I begged for coins from the tourists to pay for your purchases."

"You know very well I pay with my own money. I have more than you do."

"I've never snooped in your checkbook to see, but I think we're both well off."

"I remember when you were poor and struggling," she said with a smile.

"I was temporarily unemployed when we ran into each other again."

"Ran into each other again? We had sex on the floor of my dressing room in Michigan. It wasn't half bad."

"Yeah, you were adequate, as I remember. But you're getting better."

"You're never going to see me in this bra," she said and stuck her tongue out.

"I'll sneak it out of your dresser and try it on."

"You do, and you'll stretch it out, so keep your hands off. I'm hungry."

"Shall we go to the food court and get something?" I asked.

"Fine with me, you're paying." She stood and waited for me.

"Oh, now I pay. What happened to all your money?"

"I'm saving it for more bras." She laughed and headed toward the food court. I got up as fast as my body would let me and followed.

Bob Moats

We had our meal and then left the mall, heading back home. Our faithful toy Yorkie, Willy, rested on Penny's lap. He stayed in the van as we shopped. He didn't mind, and the van was big enough for him to run around. It was a Class B motorhome, built on a van body so it looked small, but inside it had a kitchen, bath, bedroom and everything in between. I had always wanted one, and bought this one while Penny and I were in Florida on my book signing tour.

I pulled into the drive and parked on the side of the garage. I had my restored 1989 Crown Vic next to my mini limo in the garage along with Penny's car, so the van stayed outside. We went into the house, and I shut off the driveway alarms and reset them. The house was on the western edge of Las Vegas and overlooked the Valley with the Vegas strip in the distance providing a beautiful view.

It was quiet in the house. Angelo had been staying in our guesthouse since he moved to Vegas, but he left just after he opened his restaurant. He wanted a place closer to his business. We missed him and all the great meals he cooked for us, especially the breakfasts. I knew he wanted a restaurant, so I offered to front the money for it, and he agreed.

It had been open about a month, and the business was doing quite well. I think his mob connections helped, and he had a number of local family members dining there now. He didn't want the place to become a hangout for the mobs, but they all respected Angelo and didn't make a fuss while they were there.

I just wanted to be sure no rival mobs rolled in and shot up the place to do a hit on some mob capo.

Lipstick Murders

My cell phone buzzed. The caller ID said it was Trapper. "Yeah, chief, what do you want?"

"Just checking in. It's been too quiet around the office this last week. Lacey and Mac went on vacation, and Tracey is having fits trying to make heads or tails of Lacey's file system. That's the most excitement we've had. You've been hiding out. I wondered if you were going to work anymore."

"I plan on coming back in. The weather has been so nice, Penny and I have been running around checking out all the sights we haven't seen since we moved here. Have you been to the new mob museum yet?"

Trapper laughed and said, "No, I had enough of that stuff when I was a boy here in Vegas. I remember my dad talking about the gangsters who were running the town back in the fifties. I don't need to be reminded."

"So what's Earl doing?" I asked.

"Haven't seen much of him. He took a case for some company to find out who's leaking company secrets."

"Ah, industrial espionage, right up his alley," I said.

"Yep. I'll let you go. Will I see you Monday in the office?"

"I'll make an effort to put in an appearance. Talk then," I said and hung up.

"Who was that?" Penny asked as she came into the living room. She sat next to me on the couch and handed me a beer.

214

"Ah, you know the way to my heart," I said as I popped the top. "That was Will. He's bored and wanted to know if I was, too."

"Well, are you?"

"Around you, I'm never bored. What do you have cooked up for tomorrow?"

"I thought we'd go to church. It is Sunday," she said with a slight smile.

I just stared at her until she laughed. "Sorry, I couldn't resist."

"It's not that I'm against religion, but there are too many out there to choose from."

"You could start your own. You are an ordained minister from that online church."

Before I could say anything in response, my cell phone buzzed again. It was Angelo. "Hey, friend, what's up?"

"How'd you and the Mrs. like a free meal? I need people in my place to fill seats. Got a special customer coming in tonight."

*

Continued in the book...

Jim Richards Family of Readers

Thanks to the following people who are now part of the Jim Richards Family of Readers. They have read a book or more and enjoyed them. They all volunteered to be included in the list. If you are a fan of the books, send me your full name and you will be included in future books. Send your name to murdernovels@bobmoats.com to be added here and on the website.

* Achim Feifel * Al Norris * Alex Wheatley * Alexandra Delporte-Wilkinson * Amy Tapia * Andrea Bryan * Anne Shepherd * Arianda Sugar * Arlene Markowski * Ashley Augustus * Audra Hall * Barbara Hughes * Barbara Sammons * Barbara Schuler * Barbara Zirger * Beth Donohue Plenskofski * Betsy Childress * Beth Gibson * Bill Sandy * Bill Tornquist * Billie-jo Collie * Boni J Rychener * Carl Bishopric * Carla Lewis * Carole Henderson * Carolyn Conroy * Carolyn Riddle-Linington * Cassy Bailey * Cathie Turner * Chad Hudson * Charlotte L Duran * Cheryl L. Everett * Cindy Ackley Nunn * Cindy Valstad * Connie Bancroft * Corinne Kay O'Daniel * Dana Robbins Chuchran * Dana Wichita * Danielle Monique * Darren Heald * Dave Travers * David Wilkinson * DeAnn Jannereth * Deanna Miller * Deb Breuker Balbo * Debbie Carter * Debbie White * Deborah Fartuch * Deborah Gauze * Deborah Sullivan * Dee King * Denise Freeman * Diana Carver * Dixie Beck * Donna Gould * Donna Thompson * Donny Minter * Doris Kight * Eddie Moore * Eric Walters * Felicia Annette Bradfield

Bob Moats

* Francine Menor * Gail Chesney * Georgiann Minster *
George Conner * Greg Colucci * Hayley Rankin * Harold
Garcia * Heidi Arnold * Irma Ranee Coy * Jacqueline
Moss * Jan Kimball * Janice Schneider * Janice Spoor *
Jennifer Redmond * Jessica Keown-Belous * Jim Beck *
Jo Boguslaw * Jo Turner * Joanne Marie Turner * John
Peiffer * John Wisbiski * Joseph Wauro * Joyce Stacy *
Joyce Trifiletti * Judy Franklin * Judy Travers * Judy
Padgett * Julie Heath * Junnahvee Benson * Karen Dahl *
Karen Grams * Karen Higham * Karen Kaiser * Karen
Meinburg Richwine * Karen Kirkman Parker * Karin
Hawkins * Karin Vasvari * Kathleen Donohue Roesing *
Kathleen Riddle-Wolfe * Kathy Hinds Moore * Kathy
Jones * Kathy Mitchell * Katie Benzler * Kay Burns *
Kelly Garcia * Ken Boggs * Keota Rodriguez * Kiera
Mccarthy * Kim Estes * Kitty Stolle * Kristie Sciler *
Kirsty Stanton * LaLonnie Scallen * Larry Morris *
Leann Parr * Lenora Scales * Leslie Marie Jackson *
Linda Forester * Linda Ingle Cox * Linda Kennerö *
Linda Magill * Lisa Bower * Liz Gibson * Lorraine
Wiman * Loretta Alexander * Lynda Bowles * Lynette
Lawrance * LuAnn Louttit * Manny Rothman * Marcia
Gibson DeWitt * Marie Calder * Marlene Bryan *
MaryLouise Kramp * Mary Lynn Gross * Megan Atkins *
Meghan Hyden * Melody Cannavan * Michael Carruthers
* Michael Dinkens * Michael Vannoy * Michelle Burns-
Mitchell * Michelle Pilcher * Micki Potter * Mike Moats
* Mimi Baur * Myrna Hecht * Nadine Sutton * Nancy
Ellen Sayre * Natalie Quine * Neena Martin * O'Della
Wilson * Pat Pollington * Pat Rohn * Patricia Jarmon *
Patricia C Trezza * Patrick Barry * Paul Lawrance *
Peggy Davis * Phyllis Bassett * Raylene Matheny *
Rebecca Collins Besner * Renee Brumley * Reta Hanna *
Reta Moats * Roberta Navarro-Harder * Sally Berneathy *
Sally Hubler * Sarah Santos * Satka Nikc * Sharon E.

Lipstick Murders

Edwards * Sharon Mangini * Sharon McMillon * Sheena Rawl * Sherry Amstutz * Shirley Alvarez * Shirley Davies * Shirley Williams * Stacie Rowe * Stephanie Conner * Steve Cullen * Susan Haughton * Susan Hesse Adams * Susan Salomon * Suzan K Chase * Taisha Cullum * Tamara Moore * Tammy Castleberry * Tammy Lynn Wood * Ted Murphy * Terri Atkins * Terri Creech * Terry Raab * Tonia Rachael Riggs-Williams * Travis Fleury-Lopez * Twyla Gawlas * Val Brooks * Walt Munsel * Yvonne Isakson *

Thank you to all these wonderful people.

Thank you for purchasing this book. I hope you enjoy it as much as I enjoyed writing it for my faithful readers. Please feel free to email me to tell me what you thought about my stories. I love hearing from the readers. I can be reached at murdernovels@bobmoats.com thanks again!

www.ingramcontent.com/pod-product-compliance
Lightning Source LLC
Chambersburg PA
CBHW070820120626
46556CB00002B/586